Death in Paris

Carl Weissner

Death in Paris

There must be idealism,
but there must also be contempt.

— *Raymond Chandler*

DOLL NO MORI   TOKYO

"I am not the author of every line in the book.
It is, like *The Braille Film*, a book by several authors,
living and dead. One of them myself."
—Carl Weissner

Published by
Doll No Mori Publishers
Shibuya-ku, Tokyo

More information
RealityStudio.org

Design
George Mattingly Design
www.mattinglydesign.com

Photo of Arc de Triomphe,
courtesy Office de Tourisme, Paris

Photo of Carl Weissner at Père Lachaise Cemetery,
Paris, July 2009, by Jan Herman

PRINTED IN JAPAN

Establishing Shot

He woke at 3 AM. Dim yellow light filled the room. Smog had descended on the city, filtering the bright lights of the hotel. The city was cast in a sinister sepia, as in a 1930s gangster movie. "I should have killed myself when it still made sense," he thought. He closed the curtains and went back to bed.

Near-Collision in the Main Character's Subconscious

The Hotel Bogotá, close to a hundred years old, had been kept in shape with an attitude of bored efficiency. Room service was non-existent, but there was a fat stream of brown water from every tap in the building, and the ceiling fans blew the sweat off your face in sheets. The hotel had two elevators whose cabins moved soundlessly through shafts of soot and axle-grease. In one of them, Gerald Lake rode down at 7:50 in the morning, and entered the ground floor Starbucks from the lobby.

At the far end, near the street exit, the familiar silhouette of a man in his mid-seventies made the small hairs on the back of his neck crackle with the voltage of pure hatred. He had always felt sure that he had killed his father ten years ago in Germany, by deliberately steering the car, with the old man in the passenger seat, into the concrete pillar of a bridge across Highway 3 near Cologne. He had been somewhat less than half conscious when firemen cut him out of the wreck with acetylene torches, his face swollen and rainbowed, coated in abrasions, bloody lips and cheeks flecked with tiny shards of glass. Before they could shove him into the EMS truck, he was in a deep coma. When he emerged from it after six months, his doctors showed him a letter with a photo of his father's grave somewhere in southern Germany. His stepbrother, Tony, who worked for a large software outfit down there, had made the arrangements and handled the paperwork.

Lake turned around unsteadily and crossed the diamond pattern of black and white marble tiles that had earned the Bogotá the dubious distinction of a San Francisco landmark. He pushed through the heavy slow-motion revolving door, turned left and started looking for a cab.

Posted by CW
Label: Doomsday Lit
December 7, 2007
3:12 am

Easy on the Starch

The Stanley X was a U-shaped motor court on the southern edge of Hunter's Point. The lobby looked like somebody's rec room from the Fifties, a narrow, low-ceilinged affair with imitation hardwood paneling, orange fabric chairs and a console TV in one corner tuned to a rerun of Rowan & Martin's *Laugh-In*. A greasy-haired kid with a peach-fuzz mustache sat behind the front desk.

The two detectives, swatting at a handful of bluebottles and bees, approached; the tall Caucasian in front, his Japanese partner bringing up the rear. The Jap was munching a whole-wheat tamale.

"And what can I do for you this afternoon, folks?" the kid sang out without looking up. He picked up a worker bee, pinched the end of her abdomen between his fingers, and pulled. A slimy, cream-colored thread emerged. This was the bee's rectum, its kidneys, or Malpighian tubules, and its intestines. "I'm an entomologist," he explained. "Conducting an anatomical inspection." He tossed the bee and picked up another. "Would you believe there's a theory that cell-phone transmissions are disrupting the bees' navigational ahm ... ah ... "

"We want the key to Room 216," said the tall detective. The kid looked up for the first time. There was a beat of awkward silence as he made eye contact, and all at once his expression got a little glitchy, as though he were searching some menu for the proper response. "Well now, I don't believe I ... "

A backhander from the tall one sent him reeling into the lefthand corner of the cubicle. "Don't get fresh with the law. It's a stupid thing to do." The detective didn't bother to flash his badge.

The clerk sort of undulated up the wall until his fingers reached the imitation cork panel with the keys. He unhooked the key to #216 and dropped it on the transom.

The Japanese detective, or was he a Korean ("Indeed I am a Chinese" —F. Kafka), snatched the key. "Don't do anything we can make you regret," he said. "In other words, don't do a fucking thing." He made two steps, then turned around with a frown on his face. "You look like a lady who takes it up the ass."

The air in the second-floor corridor was thick with a pasty, fibrous odor like old, spent carpet. As they neared the door of Room 216, there was a smell as though a grease fire had recently broken out in one of the rooms. "C'mon," said the tall one impatiently, "make with the key, Kawasaki-san." His slant-eyed partner put the key in the lock and opened the door. The detectives gloved up and went in.

It wasn't the unexpected spaciousness of the room, or the two queen-sized beds pushed against the north wall, one of them unmade, its blankets bunched at the foot. It wasn't the grouping of overstuffed chairs and work-desk in one corner, with the little veneer mini-bar in the other. It wasn't even the air, which had a terrible pungent closeness to it, a musty stench like wet fur, petrified chicken chow mein and mouldy newspapers. No, it wasn't any of these things that first set off the silent alarm in the detective's brain.

It was the array of photos, glossy black-and-white prints and images clipped out of magazines, taped and hung and squeezed into every available inch of wall, desk top and counter space. Photos of women.

There were other items among the photos, scattered throughout the room: Old dog-eared folders and portfolios, notebooks worn down by endless scribbling and fiddling, stacks of magazines and newspapers. The Jap detective walked over to the unmade bed and saw a manila folder lying open on the rumpled sheets. More photos. He poked around with his index finger and stopped. "Oh shit," he said in a low voice.

"What," said the tall one who was sorting through a stack of videotapes on the mini-bar.

The photo showed a woman lying on a hardwood floor, nude, one of her breasts flayed open with a metal speculum.

"If that isn't the girlfriend of our Hungarian perp."

"Czech."

"Yeah right. Roger 'n' out."

"No . . . "

"You didn't even look, you arrogant, heathen, ah ah . . . !"

"No. Listen. C-z-e-ch. As in Czechoslovakian."

"Well, the Czechs picked an unfortunate name. Why not The Shits. Easier to spell."

The tall detective had come over and stood next to his partner looking at the picture. "Tell you what. I'm going to sign up for membership in the International Ed Gein Fan Club first thing in the morning."

He recalled the awesome scene in the shy little Wisconsin farmer's home: Headless corpses hanging upside-down in the kitchen, chairs upholstered with human skin, shoeboxes full of female genitalia . . .

The detectives went through the place side by side, doggedly and systematically. None of the other photos showed a face they knew. When they opened the bathroom door with some difficulty, they got hit by a stench that suggested a thawing mummy. They reeled back and called for hazmat suits.

Let Me Bum a Ride Here

There were no cabs. Just as well. A cabbie had once quoted Raymond Chandler at him: "Places want us to go to them. They have their tongues hanging out waiting to be said." He stopped the next car on his side of the street, a black Subaru, told the woman to move over, drove down Market Street and onto the Freeway. The woman was too scared to open her mouth. Just cringed and gasped for air.

That creep Tony. Never could stand him. Probably found a

lookalike and paid him serious money to fly to San Francisco and sit in that corner every morning until I walk in. Practical joke. His idea of. Herr im Himmel. He knows I'm staying at the Bogotá, it's been in the papers. Successful crime writer in town for a bit of research.

He had picked the B. because of the lobby —the tiles had been removed from Hitler's chancellery in Berlin on orders of a General in the Army Corps of Engineers, who bought the hotel in 1946.

Herr Lake. A virus with shoes. I'll take care of him one of these days. However, first things first. Few more calls to make.

He gave no warning before cutting across three lanes of traffic to the exit ramp. They fell off the freeway like a brick dropped in water. He drove the car into an abandoned shed. It was dark inside except for a swath of sunlight that penetrated through a hole in the roof. He turned to his wide-eyed passenger. "Here's where you're supposed to shriek."

The Venceremos Hustle. Check It Out.

The shed, with the Subaru in it, burned to the ground. The moderately mutilated body of the woman driver was sold to a rich necrophile on Yerba Buena Island. By the new kids on the block: The Salvadoran Fuerzas Armadas de Hunters Point (FAHP). They ran Treasure Island, next door to Yerba B., which consists entirely of landfill contaminated with asbestos, plutonium and other carcinogens. Also, there is the high risk of liquefaction during an earthquake. It's their kind of place.

Their HQ is the abandoned gas station at Avenue N and 10th Ave., and they party (if that should be the word for the ghastly goings-on) in the Navy's former experimental contamination/decontamination lab in Area 12, which is off limits because of a high radium level.

They commuted by speedboat between the Island and their home turf, large areas south and east of McLaren Park. Their fighters were everywhere, patrolling, running things. "Doing the Extortion Shuffle" in the words of El Negro, a jefe with an education. Picture a place where it costs you ten bucks to hang a left, that'll give you an idea.

Gerald Lake decided to spend a thousand dollars on a weekend, including speedboat transfer, on Treasure I. He had never killed anyone in the middle of San Francisco Bay.

He waited for an hour on a makeshift pier made of driftwood, car wrecks and ancient beams jutting out from the northern shore of the little peninsula east of Candlestick Park. When he saw them roaring across South Basin, the sun was low, coloring the choppy sea dark silver with streaks of rust and vermilion.

They climbed out of the speedboat with their weapons propped on their hips and their faces expressionless. Two of them carried heavy machine guns with the ammunition belts draped across their bare chests. Some wore plaid skirts, others shorts or Army surplus camouflage. One was naked except for his ammunition and a pair of white Calvin Klein briefs.

They had painted their faces with chalk to signify purity and tied amulets around their arms, necks and foreheads for protection from bullets. They were a collection of walking nightmares, and when confronted with them, National Guard troops had been known to drop their weapons and run.

Their leader was a slender boy wrapped in a red turban and white robe who was helped out of the boat almost like a child. Leaders are often chosen by their god of war, and leadership can change daily. All of them skip sex during times of war, and fast to increase their powers. Those powers include the ability to drink battery acid without harm.

The Malt, the Mold
and the Monoxide

Look up "desolation" in the dictionary, what do you see? A picture of The Farout FAHP Flophouse's front lobby at 10 PM: Long shadows on the scarred parquet floor (it used to be an NCO club) from the cracked front windows, silhouettes of pale streetlights outside on the deserted corner, a single dented pay phone mounted on the lime-green cinderblock wall to your left as you come in, an ice machine cobwebbed with disuse. What you can't see is the drone of the faulty

fluorescent tubes, the monoxide clouds wafting over from the drag races on Avenue N, the mold that grows everywhere, the brewery odor emanating from the rusty vats in Area 12. —— The front desk was a cage. The mesh window sat on the painted particle-board counter. Handwritten signs all around in blunt magic marker:

NO PERSONAL CHECKS
and
BARF YR HEART OUT, ROBT. LOUIS STEVENSON.

A wire-encased fan sat rattling in one corner, circulating the stale air.

The desk was manned by a tall Jamaican with voluminous dreadlocks. "Let me guess," he said when Gerald L. rested his right elbow on the counter. "You have come to The Island for a lungful of toxins and a chance to purify your mind."

"Actually, no. But now that you mention it . . . I guess it should be comparatively easy to purify one's mind in a shitty place like this."

The Rastafarian beamed. "Ain't that just right!"

Mr. L. made an inspection tour of the island on foot and noted that, in addition to the FAHP, it was populated by college students, assorted riffraff and former homeless people—the city had provided them with a job-training center which they loved to visit whacked out of their skulls and snickering.

Midnight found him sitting cross-legged on an overstuffed chair in the alcove of his room on the top floor looking at the pixel lights of the city in the distance and reciting the names of places in the Algerian desert from memory. It was the only esoteric gimmick in his portfolio. "Tamanrasset. Tibesti. Ténéré. Tamesna. Tanezrouft. Tidjéridjaouine. Tassili-n-Ajjer. Tin Ezzararine. Tin Zouzane. Tin Ezzarirène. Tehéréguéllé. Tikoubaouine. Timesseradjen. Tainanouine. Isn't that the name of the planet where Han Solo has the Millenium Falcon reconditioned? Sorry . . . "

A Useful Aberration: Wolfman Jerry

Saturday morning he skipped breakfast and did a recon instead. He didn't see any women of the age group he was after. There seemed to be a lot of barefoot teens. On the lee side of the island there was a condemned floating casino that called itself The Fuck-off Yacht.

There was a garbage dump cum garbage processing plant. There were bonfires with goats on spits over the flames. He encountered some hardcore liquefactionists who greeted him with a hearty "I have seen the future of your armpits —salt lick for my goats!"

There was a Salvadoran child gang that forced you, at knifepoint, to give up your running shoes. There was rumored to exist on the blighted island a defrocked Pentecostal minister who came out only at night and kept yelling "Do what thou wilt —that is The Law!"

At the northwestern point of the island there was a tattoo parlor with a spectacular view of Alcatraz. The distance was approx. two miles. "Anyone ever swim over?" he asked the yakuza-type full-body ornament that owned the place. "No. You'd be the first . . . "

"Right."

The bathroom mirror at sunup had confronted him with the fact that he now looked like Chet Baker a year before he jumped out of that window in Amsterdam.

I can swim to Alcatraz on a dare, he told himself, and I'll still be your average psychopath who kills women and writes the occasional book. Never mind that I have to kill women because my French mother kept me at the bottom of a hole twenty feet below the kitchen floor and pelted me with crackers and offal twice a day. —— However. Hitler killed six million and remained a jerk. Attila the Hun offed countless folk and yet remained a narrow neurotic from the sticks. You have graduated from a wolf child cripple to a skilled criminal, from an eyesore to an hombre invisible with a talent for telling nasty stories rather well. You have no right to hope for more than that, and the duty of the dangerous mind is to become more dangerous. Isn't that what Cioran said on French television? No, he said the duty of the lonely person is to become even lonelier. But I am not lonely. I am alone, but not lonely. Loneliness, love, happiness, and all the rest of it —products of dual mammalian structure, religiously enforced two-ness. I am not two. I am one. In time. Metal time. Radioactive time. *Lycanthropos habilis.* Pshaw.

I'm Watergate Sally. Do Me.

Killing, as some wit once remarked, probably in *The New Yorker*, is like getting married. After the first time . . . Gerald L. has no use for this type of wisdom. He knows that there is misdirected sexual energy that leads to murder and mayhem. There is misdirected piety, except that piety as such is already pernicious. It's really endless.

He meditates all afternoon in the alcove of his room, with his back to the windows. Toward seven, instead of feeling hungry, he is getting horny. He unpacks an object like a fat 6 ft air mattress. It contains his reusable "victim."

He has learned to prefer Ersatzhandlung-Sex (he likes the Freudian sound of it) to the so-called real thing, and likes to reenact sex scenes from pulp novels, largely for the quaint stage directions and dialog. A Japanese expert has modified for him a sex robot built by First Androids (Nuremberg) so that the doll can produce exciting sounds when he strangles her, while a device in her abdomen enables her to buck like an artificial bull.

The thin coat of lipstick melted under my tongue. She opened her mouth wide and a stream of air from her lungs raced inside me. Her skin gave off a warm and musky smell. I nipped at her skin with my teeth and she squirmed beneath me. I rubbed back and forth between her buttocks until I felt the wrinkled opening, warm and moist like a sea anemone, begin to throb. She gasped and raised herself on her elbows and said in a hoarse voice: "Moins vite. Doucement, doucement..."

"Nix," I said. "Let's get the cows to Abilene." I pushed into her. A sharp intake of breath, then she relaxed and exhaled and I pressed as far into her as I could go.

She moaned and pressed her face into the pillow, her fingers clawing at the edges of the mattress. "Ah, c'est le max. C'est hallucinant."

I reached across her belly, my fingers sliding into the dampened fold of flesh beneath, and the sounds from her throat became very hoarse and urgent. I started kissing and biting her neck and then my lips were against the metal of the rings that ran through her ear. She had her hair thrown back, her rolled-up eyes as pale as old ivory. I had no idea what I was saying.

She gasped in her throat and then thrashed and yelled, and as she came I let myself go. A jolt of pure electricity raced through me and my cock threw up. I collapsed onto her slippery back, panting, and made a half-hearted attempt at strangling her...

The death throes, for his money, are not quite successful enough. "Plus," he says to himself, "before she signs off, I want her to say in a dying voice: 'You want a drink?'"

Say Hello to Minnesota Fats

"We're chasing a hologram," said the Japanese detective during lunch break at Le Trou, on Guerrero.

"Worse," said the tall Caucasian. "A figment . . . "

"Aw, that's so cute. Cut-oh!"

Cannibals Have No Cemeteries

Gerard Lane (since his identity is so uncertain, it is perhaps best to think of him as GL23, one of the Defense Intelligence Agency's failed human-machine-interface experiments in bilocation) and his expensive air mattress returned to the Hotel Bogotá. He had decided that life among God's bottom-feeding goldfish was not for him. Him and them being too much alike.

It had been a rough return trip. When he climbed out of the speedboat he bowed, right hand touching his forehead, in the direction of the red-turbaned boy leader of the day who had saved his life when he got sick and two hysterical streetfighters tried to throw him overboard.

The depressing news on Sunday had been that Farrah Fawcett was getting eaten alive by an anal tumor which had started to attack her liver. It didn't help that, in a tabloid photo, she looked like a million bucks and her sunglasses were sensational. He had a soft spot for the actress because of her performance in the movie where she manages to subdue and lock up the intruder who has just raped her.

At the MUNI 102 bus stop across the street some Latino teens with a ghetto blaster did the Crip Hop to Maggie Estep's "Fuck me! and take out the garbage! feed the cat and FUCK ME! You can do it! I know you can! . . . "

Why do you keep asking for it, he thought. What's wrong with you. Don't you know that you, too, can buy freedom from bad sex and untimely death for the price of a Hitachi vibrator, $68.90 plus sales tax. Get a life.

Monday morning as he entered Starbucks from the lobby, the Dead Ringer was sitting at the same table near the street exit. He stopped behind him, pulled up a chair, turned it around, straddled it and dug his middle finger into the soft tissue beneath the man's collarbone where twenty-six individual nerves join into the brachial plexus. The man made a high-pitched buzzing moan. Veins jumped in his neck, and tears streamed over his face.

The place was crowded and loud. When GL23 finally released the pressure, the man sagged and his face paled to the color of meat left in water.

"You will not survive our next encounter," he said close to the man's left ear. "So make sure it never happens." He paid for a Sportsman cookie the size of an old 33 1/3 rpm single on his way out. "I'm using up too many guilty walk-ons," he muttered to himself.

Tape Will Self-Destruct in Five

On his way to City Lights for the ritual stealing of a book
—he did it every time he came to town—he passed the
black skeleton of the old Kaiser warehouse. It had been,
six months ago and for a persuasive fee, one of his more
ambitious arson jobs. He had been undecided for a long
time before he'd convinced himself that life as an arsonist
was not his karma.

He had fond memories of the day he stole a copy of Bukowski's *Notes of a Dirty Old Man*, on display just to the left
of the narrow staircase that led to the second floor, and
read half of it that same afternoon in the Hang Ah Tea
Room near Sacramento and Stockton. 1 Pagoda Place was
the address, a tiny alleyway; it was slightly underground,
space was limited, no waitresses pushing dim sum carts
around, in business since 1920. After some spectacularly
ill-conceived retrofitting, it had since turned into a tourist
trap with sturdy plastic chairs that had the same color as
the Golden Gate Bridge.

City Lights Bookstore seemed larger than he remembered
it. It had a fresh coat of creamy paint, but inside you still
walked on the same torn checkerboard linoleum. On the
wall next to the *poste restante* space there had always been
a printed sign announcing "God Is Coming, And Is She
Pissed." It had been replaced with a handwritten ad for a
female rapper's CD: "Shoot yr shit sky-high and come on
my thigh . . . !"

There was a book case labeled "Aryan Lit. (know your en-

emy)". Other racks and shelves offered White Supremacy /
Black Supremacy / The Bourne Supremacy. Religion. Fire-
arms and Silencers. Manga. Bomb-Making. Poetry. Bio-
logical Warfare. Torture, Confidence Games and Organic
Gardening shared the same window space.

G. felt momentarily tempted to liberate a copy of *The Homeless Person's Cookbook*. It contained a lot of tongue-in-cheek
stuff like Turdburgers, etc. He decided against it. Leave it
for the truly needy.

By the time he reached 631 Grant, his feet hurt. His agent,
Bruno "Il Brigante" Alioto, for some reason had fallen in love
with the Far East Café, which had been operating for more
than eighty years and still had private wooden booths with
curtains (it had started out as an opium den, according to
Bruno). The agent also represented Charlie Huston who wrote
about the vampire clans of Manhattan. ("Whenever I need to
get his attention, all I say is 'Huston, we have a problem . . . '")

The oldest waiter on the premises served genuine shark's
fin soup ($120 a bowl), working his eyebrows up and down
and uttering what sounded like a melodious threat.

G. finally looked up. "I might throw your guts out the window one day," he said equably. "Think about it."

The waiter seemed pleased. He turned around and vanished.
Old Chinese waiters often presume that instead of learning
how to speak English it is their natural privilege to pass
remarks in some hick dialect.

"I have been thinking," said Bruno, "about your idea of the
demented ex-sniper who is terrorizing Paris by doing a

Charlie Starkweather in every one of the twenty arrondissements, on successive days, without getting caught. Which
he achieves by stashing twenty rather good rifles in twenty
attics around town . . . That's an expensive gig."

"Yeah, but it works."

Twin Creeps

The criminal life, by and large, is a pain in the ass. There
is a percentage in it, but since it has no future, and you can
feel the heat closing in, and have to keep looking over your
shoulder . . . forget it.

G. decided that since he had a choice, he should perhaps
elect to live off his royalties, and with a criminal past.

At this point his twin brother starts terrorizing Paris. Not
his twin in Second Life, pursued by the SL Police Paral-
lèle, but his real twin, in real time. Which is exasperatingly
inconvenient. Only the twin is doing it with improvised
explosive devices, keeping it simple. His MO essentially
consists of tossing parcels into cafés and movie theaters
with a perfunctory "Plastique . . . "

The twin, who calls himself Bernd Norton (no pun intend-
ed), doesn't look like him, or himself, anymore because
he is addicted to crystal meth: He is concocting it in his
bathroom, and the acetone keeps blowing up in his face.
With the result that he looks more like the twin brother of
Mickey Rourke in that movie, what's it called . . . This really
complicates things but it cannot be helped.

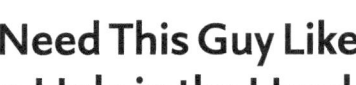

Need This Guy Like a Hole in the Head

GL23 objects to this turn of events, so . . . back to 631 Grant Ave. —— "Everybody's picking on Paris," says Bruno. "Why? There's Düsseldorf . . . Last week I saw a synopsis where bacteria that feed on iron have escaped from a military installation in Poland and are cutting a path of destruction across Europe, aiming for the Eiffel Tower . . . "

G. looks at him and yawns. The ancient waiter serves the Egg Foo Yong.

Bruno is on a roll. "Look at all the railway bridges . . . train is nearing bridge . . . will they make it crumble in time? . . . cliffhanger every half hour . . . "

G. is getting impatient. "I'm not in the business of competing with bacteria. Porca Madonna . . . "

Eh, Paisán. Paso de Ganado.

"They's suppose to be countless ways of being dead. Believe me, they's only one." —El Zorro in SURF NAZIS MUST DIE——— In the dusky office of a derelict warehouse on Howard Street, the Triad negotiator crossed his legs, showing off his tasseled oxblood oxfords. The FAHP lieutenant standing next to him, naked except for a pin-striped cutaway coat, mechanically kicked the offending foot back down to the grimy floor, while the boy with the turban frowned at a sheet of paper with Chinese characters and a typed column that read like Pidgin English in phonetic spelling.

The tall sliding door was pulled open maybe a foot or so and a thin boy who looked a lot like the turbaned child leader squeezed sideways through the narrow opening. He had soiled white bandages around his wrists and neck.

"Get the bleeder out of here," said the war god's mouthpiece tonelessly, without looking up. "He pigstyed my bedroom with arterial spray."

A Silo Fulla Corn Where This Came From

On this day, shortly after 4 PM, G. and the two detectives were, for several minutes, within sight of each other, at a distance of less than a hundred yards. He was standing at a window on the second floor of the New Riviera Hotel, and the detectives were in Washington Square, the tall one spooning Bami Goreng from a biodegradable container, and his Japanese partner munching a soggy BLT. They would never come this close again.

There will never be, next-door to the Wonder Food Co. on Waverly Place, an office coordinating the efforts of FAHP and the Thousand Points of Light Triad. Instead, there will be an epidemic of ritual killings on both sides, lasting several months.

Mutilated bodies of women, of a certain age group, will command less and less attention and ultimately drop below the radar of Robbery-Homicide. GL23 senses that right now the risk of getting caught at anything except mass slaughter of Chinese hoodlums is probably lower that what it would be in Lagos, Nigeria. Maleesh.

Yes, Muyster Dyalin'

"I know a guy who witched out a well in San Anselmo last spring," says the Jap.

"Do you have to talk like Festus? You're so pathetic, Kemos-abe."

They are sitting in a porn movie basement clip joint in the Tenderloin, and the movie is putting them in a state close to hibernation.

"Besides, you can't ah ah disassociate yourself from the existing water supply . . . "

"I know. The ShvartzeNigger will not let you."

"That's an affirmative."

"What I mean is we need to bring in a Ted Serios type . . . "

"Yeah, right. Ted could of thunk a picture of your perp into an old SX-70 Polaroid Camera justlikethat . . . " The tall one snaps his fingers. "Jesus, gimme a break."

A person sitting somewhere to the left of them turns around and makes a hissing sound. The tall one leans left and whacks the guy across the face. "You're under arrest. Assume the position. We can show you a good time, Jerkoff."

Mutants Beat Their Meat in the Street

Outside the Abandoned Planet Bookstore on Valencia, an idiot juggler kept twelve flaming torches in the air with the aid of a rudimentary third arm growing out of his chest. G. found a book on cannibalism. He liked the title: DIVINE HUNGER.

G. walked through the narrow twisting streets of the Quarter —the Vista Point City Guide called it "The Android Jungle" —past vendors selling charms and jewelry, and carts loaded with unsanitary looking food. Mongoloid punks wheeling around in a gynecologist's chair looked at him with huge mournful eyes. There was a row of rainbow-colored brothels. Waves of unknown stench filled the streets.

He turned a corner and stopped. A tall ragged old man with a cane was blocking his way. The skin had grown smooth and hairless over the socket where his left eye should have been.

"You wish the services of a genuine scanner?" he asked.

G. nodded.

"Follow me," said the mutant.

The two detectives got out of the car opposite VD COMIX, hurried past the telemeters and Time Clocks, walked up to the Console and faded through an invisible turnstile. They pushed through clusters of temporal agents checking in & out of time flicks, picked up on 1970 and saw talked felt

were film . . . Subway train roaring through a crumbling
mosque . . . A clan of black whores laughing and holler-
ing "Time Machine! Field Kit, Baby!" . . . Connor and Elvis
Arakawa barged into the hot flesh and wound up in a motel
in Daly City registered under false names and burned . . .
Connor went outside to take a look and didn't like what
he saw . . . CLEVELAND SKYVIEW MOTEL . . . Jesusfuck-
enchrist, dove siamo . . . He went back inside and reached
across the front desk . . . "Where's my partner?!" . . . "Kattar
Kheirak! . . . cuidado . . . you can be traced . . . "

Dee Enemy

The graffiti writers of FAHP are keeping busy. This isn't
taggers out to get famous all over town, it's gangbangers
marking turf and making challenges and telling you who
they have killed and who they're going to kill. There is, from
time to time, a brief spell of silliness ("I got the dinero, go
fetch the Camaro!") It helps them to stay sharp.

The kids manning the roadblocks have seen it all, and their
life-expectancy is lower than that of the rest (17.5). They
stand and lean, eyeing the stranger with a sullen confronta-
tional stare, their voices slow from years of smoking heroin.
Their favorite rock groups are Kid Congo & The Brutal Mon-
key Birds, Alien Ant Farm, and Vendetta Red.

They have names like Mad Max, Yul (a shaved head), Cool
B, Shala, Porkin' Louie, Dee Enemy. Some wear US-flag
bandannas. Around their necks hang leather thongs with

polished wooden or stone amulets. Carved fetish figurines stand guard alongside their roadblocks.

A girl commander stands out: She is wearing glittering gold jeans rolled to the calf, six-inch platform shoes, and a dun-colored T-Shirt with "Godzilla's m' dawg" emblazoned on it in silver letters that glow in the dark.

For the rest of the month, the war god has chosen a gimpy 6 ft 1 warrior who walks the noon streets with a hyena on a leash.

A Jane Doe has been found in the Bay.

Vuelvete y Aganchete, Pendejo

The FAHP have a Celtic necromancer on retainer. Their former guy, a Guatemalan witchdoctor, gave them one bum steer too many. The nec's first job is to get in touch with the dead and put a potent spell on the National Guard unit —heavy machineguns and armoured personnel carriers —bivouaking in Crocker Amazon Playground.

The Triad negotiator has been tarred and feathered, then quartered and delivered to Waverly Place in four identical shabby suitcases. There was a dissing remark by a Triadista on KRON-TV. With the result that Chinese body parts lit-tered several parks and alleys.

During off-duty hours, the indios among the FAHP fighters love to watch reruns of Bonanza. It generally takes less than a minute before they start pelting the screen with chicken bones and crushed beercans.

The TPL Triad mounts a two-pronged attack, simultaneously firebombing the gas station HQ on Treasure Island and the warehouse on Howard Street. Limited number of casualties on both sides.——The beautiful 16-year-old Chinese twins working afternoons in their parents' stationery and office supply store on Kearny get hacked to death.

Something breaks inside the tall detective. "I've seen a lot of blood and insanity," he says in a tired voice, "but this is worse than the Old Testament. We can't win . . . "

Elvis Arakawa felt embarrassed. His partner never showed any emotions except anger and disgust. Never.

C'est le Darkness

"Persons who arouse his suspicion," he notes about the main character of his next book which will have a motto from Sayaan Supa Crew, a hiphop group in Marseille: "C'est le Darkness."

Watch for them long enough and you are bound to enter the poisonous aura of one who will lash out at you. Or, if it's a near miss, who will attack someone right in front of you . . . A cul-de-sac in a riverside park becomes a killing ground; a front stoop serves as the stage for a conversation that triggers a revenge killing; a tavern with a back door opening on a deserted stretch of waterfront will be the site of an execution . . . The drab places acquire an icky phosphorescent taint from what has happened in them. He finds it impossible to change the channel on his reality or navigate a way out of these streets and buildings that bind him to the others . . . in ways dictated by what? Mektoub, hombre. It is written.

There is a character in an apartment on the other side of the street watching something on TV . . . he gets up, walks around . . . his movements blur . . . suddenly, he is in sharp focus . . . with a hardon he has been carrying from room to room like a divining rod . . . now he beats off furiously . . . It's Julio Cabeza, a member of the Norteno gang in South San F., sought for attempted murder. It will take them almost a year to find him. Why? He has become another. He lives in a world that is too dark for them. It has the disturbing effect of a permanently unresolved moment in a parallel present which refuses to settle into a satisfying final image. There is no way you can account for this in a police report. No se puede mirar. One cannot look at this. Francisco Goya.

300 Pounds
of Lesbian Bed Death

Armed HipHop Comes to Chinatown. The San Francisco Chronicle, below the fold. Above, there is the war in Somalia and the fact that S.F. has become the capital of Techno-Yech, with bands like Ugly Niggahs in Ugly Clothes, Buttfucked

Slasher Bimbos, The Seppukku Chihuahuas, De Awesome Shitbirds.

A furious Senator from Santa Barbara, her thin lips the color of old liver, demands a vote to impeach the governor. She also demands martial law for the entire Bay Area. ("Do you want to shilly-shally until the headline is 'Urban Warfare —This Is Not A Drill!' ")

The warrior jefe with the hyena is quoted, in the Oracle-Guardian, with a blunt statement: "I don't have a bullet-proof vest, but I can drink acid. Can you drink acid? I can drink acid. We are a world power. We are waiting. Fuck you, Jewish degenerates, bottom-feeding ah ah . . . "

G. folds the paper and shoves it under his left arm. The lift operator is a gelatinous giant somehow reminiscent of Babe McCloor in D. Hammett's "Flypaper." He surveys GL23 with beady eyes the color of sewage. "Keep your nose clean, shamus," he says, "or I'll sit on your face."

In the street there is the familiar smell of putrid carrot mush and carrion.

Man Finds Condom in Burger

On this sun-drenched Saturday afternoon he catches a glimpse of the banner headline of yesterday's Bay City Sentinel seconds before it becomes fishwrap: READ THIS AND WEEP, BRAD . . . A carpet of plastic garbage the size of

Oregon is floating, and slowly circling, halfway between San Francisco and Hawaii!!

Another fifteen years, he mumbles to himself, and in the south-eastern part of the Bay, maybe in the estuary of a failed river, you'll have a floating slum called Lagos Lagoon, recently awarded the prestigious title of Aspirational Shantytown of The Year . . . Thousands of driftwood and cardboard shacks, perched on stilts a few feet above their own bobbing refuse, with rust-never-sleeps scrapmetal roofs wreathed in the smoke and haze from thousands of cooking fires. Market women and teenage crack dealers will paddle plastic and birchbark canoes on water as black and viscous as an oil slick.

Back at the hotel, in an ill-advised attempt at mood management, he checks out the website of 4Wheel Sexdrive, Ltd., Tokyo, a manufacturer of artificial-intelligence sex robots ("fembots") . . . "Our A.I. Neo is a dynamic 158cm tall . . . natural posing due to a new single axis on a double joint which allows for 33 degrees of increased movement . . . The Neo-J is a sleek 154cm body type with real and moderate slender girl deformation . . . "

Crippled fembots that'll give you lip . . . for the handicapped and seriously kinky male customer . . . no stone remains unturned.

"One head is included per doll, although additional heads may be ordered, at $735 per. In order to transplant the feel of real woman's breasts to our dolls, a new special elastomer-gel is enclosed in a breast. They are more humane then breasts of our old model! $5,425 plus shipping charges."

And here is the new Piston Robot: "This self-heating dildo ($300) takes thirty minutes to get to body temperature. The machine's multispeed controller runs from one to 150 strokes per minute . . . "

The gPod Dildo has three independent motors which vibrate in time to any audio input, including the sound of the human voice. "The name is as ingenious as the design: A triple pun on iPod, G-spot and the Japanese character for masturbation —jii. Perfect for long-distance relationships (connected to a phone)!"

There is a link to a report from Japan's First Sex Show . . . a Shibuya-based S&M porn-video company has staged live shows at intervals during the day . . . one featured a woman with her clothes torn to shreds, hung by the wrists from a scaffold and tortured "at strategic points" by men wielding chunky vibrators and tasers . . . ——Waterbondage . . . a hat so old the ancient Egyptians sneered at it . . . Slaves Bound and Dunked . . . You should have seen my water bill last month . . . ——Ah . . . Men in Pain: Men's faces fucked with dirty women's feet before having their asses violated . . . right . . . "As long as I have a face, you'll always know where to stamp your feet, Sweetmeat . . . " ——I might as well try to make my Frollein Liselotte of Nuremberg last a little longer . . . There is a writer in Frankfurt, former airline pilot, who has been writing about sex with replicants for more than forty years . . . and has yet to encounter one . . . must be maddening . . . wonderful writer . . . in a class by himself . . . and so to bed . . .

They Ride by Night

There has been a mass breakout from the Army nuthouse in the Presidio which gave under an onslaught of kudzu. Some of the Living Dead now wandering the streets are more than a hundred years old and have seen action at Omaha Beach and Bastogne.

"What's he saying?"

"He is trying to ah deliver a tune by the Andrews Sisters: 'An'-An' he's the boogie-woogie bugle boy of Company B!'"

"You're shitting me."

"Afraid not."

Bad Lieutenant

The Captain, corn starch caked under his balls, is sitting at his desk sideways, crossing and uncrossing his legs as though a bad itch won't let him feel at home in his swivel chair. "In other words, you got bupkes."

"Guy's a fuckin' insect," says Connor.

"No, he isn't. Or we would be the Entomology Department. Which we ain't." A mirthless chuckle escapes his bluish lips. He produces an ugly-looking gob from his right nostril, rolls it between thumb and forefinger and pings it against the lieutenant's crotch. "Dismissed."

Death Comes to McNulty

9 AM. In a cantina near the corner of 16th and 6th, he orders Caffé Bustelo and huevos rancheros and checks the competition . . . "The sun was dipping below the Suleiman Range as the car swung off Jamrud Road west of the airport. The Company had a high-walled villa sandwiched between the estate of a Pashtun drug dealer and a warehouse filled with artificial limbs."

Right. Another one starring the aficionados of cause and effect. The arrogant envoys of the pickle factory, with their purposeful stride and the ability to remain indifferent to failure. Who wrote this one? The Brit? No, the Australian. My Aussie pursuer, who hasn't left Coober Pedy in twenty years, is gaining on me . . .

Outside, in an improvised game of soccer, three kids are kicking a dead kitten around.

A black National Guard humvee with AIM TO PLEASE, SHOOT TO KILL stencilled on its side, slowly rounds the corner . . .

11:30 AM. At Get Lost Books, 1825 Market St., he buys a copy of Eric Hazan's "L'invention de Paris". He is looking forward to writing the Paris sniper story on location, and one can never know enough about the history of certain *quartiers*.

He spends an hour writing in his room, and the rest of the afternoon meditating on the roof of the Bogotá.

At approx. 6:15 PM, Walter McNulty, a homicide dick in the

Sheriff's Office, finds his Japanese wife with her throat cut, hands tied behind her back, feet lashed together with grey duct-tape. She is sitting on the kitchen floor in the couple's Potrero Hill apartment, leaning against the north wall. A comet's tail of arterial splatter has shot across the wall and trickled down in dozens of tiny rivulets. Her chin is resting on her chest. A fortune cookie is sticking to her forehead. Carotid artery and trachea have been severed. She has lived long enough to see her blood spray outward in an arc, to aspirate blood into her severed windpipe, to hear it gurgle in her lungs, and to cough it out in bursts of crimson phlegm . . .

At ten minutes of eight, G. briefly remembers a woman he had to pick up in a bar in order to kill her. She loved to talk. "I dragged a guy home once, back when I was still sleeping with strangers, y'know, he was about your age and incredibly good-looking and just sensational in bed, and he'd never been married, either. I couldn't figure it until I found out he was a priest . . . "

"I'm not a priest."

"That's a shame. You could be a trouble-shooter for God."

He had put her out with a blast of formaldehyde from an 8oz. atomizer. The insides of her thighs showed a grey lace-like pattern; the skin of her arms and legs appeared thickened and, in places, callused like the sole of a foot. He read up on it and found that it was caused by an allergy to certain kinds of tropical timber.

He stands at the open window of his room until the last rays of daylight have left; until the lights of the city reflected off the cloud cover and the sky outside the window turn a dull industrial henna.

It occurs to him that the movie of his life is so linear, and so easily told, that in the end not many celluloid scraps will litter the cutting-room floor.

Esperan. Estan Testigos.

"I was 12 when they kidnapped us, and my brother was ten. They killed my brother and cooked him with manioc and told us to eat of him. If you refused, you got your head split with a machete. It took us three days to eat him. Fué duro. It was hard. Then they broke camp and moved us deeper into the jungle."

A FAHP child soldier ostensibly seeking refuge in the Catholic church at Haight and Laguna. Bruno Alioto tries to sign him up on the spot.

Elvis Has Just Left the Building

"Here's what I found going through the notebooks of the ah slain Salvadoran madam that was discovered this morning at oh-six-hundred in one of the trash cans outside her uh établissement," says Elvis Arakawa . . . "At one end of the stage, under a hard white light, a Thai woman is reclining on a lawn chair. On either side of her there's a girl in sequined panties holding one of her ankles. The woman makes a bellowing noise and thrusts her hips. The girls seem to be pulling her ankles like levers. A dart flies from her cunt across the stage into a target. Cheers erupt from the Chinese businessmen . . . "

We Can Offer You an Ejector Seat at the Amok Koma Disaster Control Training Center

The FAHP graduate to mortars. The oppressor state gets another chance and blows it. A National Guard platoon gets wiped out in the Castro. "You Never Saw Faggots Fight with Such Ruthless Determination," it says across the front page of The Advocate.

A Chinese suicide bomber walks into the Tora Bora, much frequented by FAHP fighters, and is detonated by remote control. The sprinkler system comes on, then a water main is severed, and a mix of blood and water is washing across the floor of the restaurant and pouring through what is left of the front and onto the wide sidewalk. It looks like a slaughterhouse being hosed down after the working day.

Ragged pieces of chairs and tables are floating past, shoes, shredded ferns and artificial gladiolas, purple and blackened body parts. Then a second detonation, from a ruptured gas main, and flames billowing across the shambles lot.

The light has turned strange as the sun is veiled by smoke and a reddish fog. There is a smell in the air which is not immediately recognizable to anyone who doesn't know war. It clogs the nostrils with powdered brick and concrete, raw sewage, open drains and a disgusting meatiness.

Doll No Mori, Shishkebab (Not a Fucking Anglo-Saxon Left in the Department)

Elvis is doing a family dinner around the corner from the Japanese Tea Garden. "I hear your partner suicided out," says one of his nephews.

"Hai! Never could stand the dyspeptic bastard."

Guffaws and A-mens all around.

A half hour later, more s'kosh, Elvis Arakawa (not his real name) breaks down sobbing and whimpering in the men's room. Four of his five nephews, dick in hand, are standing around him feeling grossed-out embarrassed.

He claws at the youngest one's thighs. "Gimme that Boy Scout knife, Billy-Bob!" he bawls. "I'm gonna commit harrah harrah . . . Harry Kirshner! . . . "

And God Said: I Got Mine! Fuck You! Every Crumb for Himself!

The ascetic Nigerian preacher who used to harangue the crowds in Washington Square now stands vow-of-silence dumb next to a huge hand-painted sign: "You are not only fucked you are doomed. You get flushed down the toilet of histery. You not be toast. You will be turds. Petrified turds to be dug up and cast aside by angry black creatures from Mars."

Circling the Drain

"A bluebird singing in every garden, and a Humvee in every house." George Clooney outlining his platform in case he should decide to run for Governor of California.

The FAHP necromancer is performing a roadside ceremony at dawn, supposedly hexing the James Lick Freeway. Most of south-eastern San Francisco below Army Street is already indistinguishable from Kigali or the bidonvilles of Port-au-Prince.

In the lobby of the Bogotá, someone had left a paperback on one of the two black leather easy-chairs. G. plopped down, opened the book at random . . . "Mulholland Drive. It's a dangerous road, home to the breached guardrail, the meandering Marlowe, the David Lynch fantasy, the 2:00 AM

drunken head-on. You'll drive it too fast and be glad you did."
Gregg Hurwitz, *I See You.*

Hm. His bad guys will find it difficult to out-ugly the
sumbitches in my books, but he's good. Time to leave the
country. You don't want to feel challenged by the stray
book left in a hotel lobby yet . . . In France I'll be up against
Grangé, and that's it.

The Murder Pace

"Seventy murders is what you got in Fort Lauderdale in 1988,"
the Captain is saying in front of a few cameras and micro-
phones. "Seventy is what you are getting now in Caracas
in a week. I think we are doing fine." The body count this
week is 38. Peachy.

In the RHD squad room his detectives are watching him on
an old wall-mounted TV set with the jitters. They are rolling
their eyes and making the sign of the cross.

Detective Arakawa remembers that one of the body movers
had blue tears tattooed at the corners of his eyes. They are
using a new outfit that calls itself HOTS (Haulers Of The
Stiffs). He finds all of this fucking hilarious.

Beat Me Daddy Eight to the Bar

"Scientists at the Polytechnic University of Cartagena (Spain) have created a sensitive robotic finger that can feel the weight of pressure it is exerting and adjust the energy it uses accordingly, allowing a robot to caress its human partner with the sensitivity of a virtuoso lover."

G. closes the tab, folds his hands behind his head and stretches. "Boy, when I want my clit diddled by a virtuoso I use an eggbeater."

Long Time Nobody Make Jump

Don DeLillo got a degree in theology and then wrote advertising copy for a while, but he never came up with this one: "You've got to feed the gods, or the gods will feed on you. Not that they won't feed on you anyway." (Bukowski) Voilà.

G. briefly thought of getting on a PSA flight to L.A., rent a suitable wreck and visit B's grave site, with a view of the ground-to-air missiles and radar dishes on the highest part of Palos Verdes Peninsula, and Terminal Island Federal Prison and the big tankers out there. An inspired epileptic who had legally changed his name to Obi-wan Kenobi had done a pike dive from the tamerack to the left of the grave and broken his neck.

Fly or Die

G. settled his hotel bill. The German fembot in its air mattress cocoon was already in storage. He was going to emulate the boys of the Fuerzas Armadas and abstain from sex during the writing of his next book. Semantic warfare was, after all, not so different from the other kind. ——Bruno had mentioned that his proofreader in New York City had died of a heart attack last Monday, and the others in the large office at HarperCollins somehow failed to notice. On Saturday morning, a cleaning woman had asked the dead man if he was going to work through the weekend. When she didn't get an answer, she shook his elbow, and he limply draped himself over the left arm rest, rigor mortis having come and gone. G. decided to dedicate the Paris novel to Paul Ingersoll, dead at 59 and rotting away in the line of duty.

Layers of fat black smoke over China Basin. Half of McLaren Park reduced to cinders. The air tasted of pencil lead. Del Shannon singing "Runaway" in somebody's car radio. These were the last blips on his radar before he boarded an Air France A-380 at ten PM.

What I Killed Today.com

Charles de Gaulle, not one of the more popular airports (half a terminal had collapsed just recently), was the usual directionless mess. G's feet (which according to his passport belonged to one Alain Laurin) hurt by the time he reached the hall where his baggage was supposed to squeeze through the slits in a sturdy plastic curtain at the feed end of the carousel. He recognized a few faces from his flight. The carousel was not moving. Time for a piss.

The men's room was deserted. To the left of the door, catering to the needs of the Japanese salaryman, there was a vending machine from which you could pull unwashed teenie panties. G. was about to finish spraying the immaculate tiles — a thin intermittent waterfall kept them fresh — when a youngish character wearing a tight Italian shirt walked in, stood next to him, reached over and fondled his dick.

G. steps behind the guy and says: "Hold still." The presumptuous perp is shivering expectantly. G. puts his left arm across the guy's chest, grabbing a fistful of shirt, and the crook of his right arm over the guy's chin and gives a violent jerk, snapping the youngman's neck. He drags the limp body of the offender into one of the stalls and makes it sit on the porcelain bowl.

He didn't ask himself if his action made any sense. In any case, JP Sartre had answered the question for him. "Si l'action réussit, le sens est inscrit." *Being & Nothingness*, page 605. Sure, it was extra work, but it was also liberating.

Around noon he emerged from the Châtelet RER station into that peculiar Parisian light which always struck him as too little, too late; and which was the reason why Jacques Monory did his photo-realist paintings of French gangsters and their victims in the coldest, most unreal-looking blue that money can buy. And wasn't it Bettina Rheims who had said: "Paris is a dull, dark city . . . I can never depend on the light, so I use strobes, klieglights and amateur flashes, even outside. Everything is relit."

He hailed a cab and said to the driver: "Sixty rue de Seine." The cabbie, after establishing that his passenger had used the RER from the airport, mentioned that G. could have stayed on the train until Saint-Michel.

G. cut him short. "I prefer to cross the river rather than burrow underneath it."

"Same here," said the driver, a Kenyan with tribal marks. ("My old man abducts tourists for money. So do I . . . hyrch, hyrch!")

G. told him to take the Pont Notre Dame rather than the Pont Neuf. Looking at the Cathedral across the Pl. du Parvis N.D., he once again thought that Notre Dame, after years of sandblasting, now looked like a plaster replica the color of chicken shit in a theme park on the outskirts of Osaka.

Meanwhile, the Kenyan was bringing him up to date. "Clamart is getting choked to death by mutated kudzu! Says here, in Le Parisien! A ten-year-old girl got ripped to pieces by two German Great Danes . . . I thought there were only German shepherds, but what do I know? Hey shit huh?"

The history of the Hotel La Louisiane at the corner of Boulevard St. Germain and Rue de Seine goes back to an officer in Napoleon's army who went AWOL and proceeded to make a fortune in the skin trade — in Louisiana. Everybody has stayed here at one time or another, from Hemingway to Nam June Paik; and Albert Cossery, an Egyptian who wrote strange novels (*Mount Analog*, *Men God Forgot*), has lived here for more than fifty years and only changed rooms once. Even in his final months on the planet, he could be seen making for his bench in the Jardin des Plantes every morning at 10.30, spindly and emaciated and with the decrepit out-of-sync walk first demonstrated by Walter Brennan in *To Have and Have Not*. And here's another one: "Between the wars, in his room at the Hotel La Louisiane, Cyril Connolly used to breed ferrets that he fed on bloody pieces of liver procured from the horse butcher's across the street. They wore harnesses with bells on." Nathalie de Saint Phalle, *Hotels Littéraires*, 1991.

G. checked in. "B'jour, M'sieu Laurin," said the receptionist. In the shade of a giant potted yucca sat a mulatto Poule de Luxe wearing a purple tank top that said FAST FLESH across her tits. An internet start-up now occupied five of the eighty rooms as well as the mezzanine above the front desk.

The elevator was condemned until further notice. G. took the stairs. They were narrow and curved, with a faded runner held in place by tarnished brass fittings. He had a reservation for room no. 7 on the second floor. It was a close, musty place — lopsided queen-size bed with a busted frame, splintered laminate nightstands, stained lamp shades, cracked plaster walls. The worn, oatmeal-colored carpeting was mildewed and damp.

The two features that made the room worth a hundred bucks a night were high-speed internet access and the fact that you had three feet of open space between your side of the bed and the wall. Instead of three inches.

As he stood at the window looking down Boulevard St. Germain toward the Carrefour de l'Odéon, a sick feeling suddenly came over him, like when a cat jumps onto your shoulder with its claws out.

If You Can Swallow a Gnat, Why Gag at a Camel

The Journal du Dimanche offers an explanation for the dead body in the men's room across from baggage claim area 6A in CDG Terminal 2: A gay paratrooper who was asking for it.

The President of the Republic reminds everyone that he has always been against gays in the military.

The Clichy-sous-Bois ayatollah issues a fatwa: "It is your duty, oh brothers, to bash the maricónes wherever you find them."

The Cardinal-Archbishop is livid: "Don't touch our differently swayed parishioners, you poisonous freak."

The Chief Rabbi, one of the coolest customers around, points out that beur hoodlums in Bagneux have killed yet another Jewish adolescent, after torturing him for a total of three days, and nobody bothered to work up a lot of adrenalin about it.

"It is noteworthy that 95% of what is reported in the French media is controlled, and often generated, by a conglomerate of arms manufacturers and banks." (*The Guardian*).

On Va Draguer le Secteur

Every night the ghost of the tall detective comes down the narrow hall, accompanied by a partner who is hard to see, he's so insubstantial and unimportant. They feel sure that they have found their man, but find it maddening that there is never any proof.

All their energy and determination has left them; they seem listless and dejected. It is obvious that they have accepted their fate: In a parallel universe, as meaningless as it is hostile, the ghost detectives are reduced to the empty gesture of going through the motions forever. Et pas de commission.

As they melt through G's door, they both snap on a pair of latex gloves. They check the doorframe, doorknob, switch plates. Given the amount of blood generated by this killer, there should be olfactory echoes, like underexposed negatives, of splatters and whorls and eddies and pools throughout the room. They find none.

They enter the bathroom and flip on the light. After a few seconds, the fluorescent fixture over the mirror flickers to life, settling into a loud hum. They poke around, lifting the toilet seat, running a gloved finger around the drain in both the tub and the sink, checking the grout in the tile around the tub and in the folds of the shower curtain. Nothing.

"I always thought," says the pale partner (of course there is no sound, but they have become expert lip readers) "that it would be like on *Law and Order.* On *L&O* they solve everything in about an hour. Less, when you cut out the commercials."

The tall one stares at him for a beat and a half. "You are so pathetic, Kemosabe, you know that?"

I Now Declare
Place d'Estienne d'Orves
a Free Fire Zone

Two days of location hunting, and the difficulties of the sniper plot are glaringly, no, "laceratingly" obvious, as his publisher likes to say. His French publisher is a Brit named Edward Lansky (no relation to the gangster) who set up shop on the Place de l'Odéon in early 1968.

Ed likes to tell the story of Emile Cioran, the Roumanian misanthrope extraordinaire, who lived in a chambre de bonne around the corner and in May '68 was asked to address the students who had taken over the Théâtre de l'Odéon. Cioran got up there and barked into the microphone: "What this country needs is a solid Entnazifizierung!" A denazification program for France was considered outré, so they booed him off the stage.

It is easy to find suitable buildings bordering a square or park where there are a lot of people and the firing range is right, but how do you get in and establish a cache in the attic and later a safe spot from which you can deliver a hail of bullets. There is hardly a building left in the city that hasn't been turned into a fortress it seems. So the sniper, a devious and ambitious nut, will devise ways; and surprise the reader, time and again, with his frightful resourcefulness. And he will always know when to ease off on his greedy drive . . . It would be unreasonable to expect the Generali Bldg., diagonally across from the Théâtre Mogador (a choice site . . .), to say uncle just because you need to put a shooter behind that convenient parapet there. And it goes without saying that the Demented One will never stoop to a drive-by shooting.

Perhaps, it occurs to G., the guy should commit his heinous acts of terror using Lee Harvey Oswald's legendary piece of mail-order shit, the Mannlicher-Carcano. That would be the ultimate insult . . . However, the Mannlicher has since become a rara avis. Leave it to André Breton. So instead, Le Snaypeur has liberated twenty FN assault rifles cal. 7,62mm as used by the armed forces of various western European countries in the sixties —several of them from the manufacturer's own museum (Fabrique Nationale, Belgium) where security had been nil, as opposed to other army museums where it had been lax.

Ed & El, a Vaudeville Team

Elvira Lansky, suffering from multiple sclerosis and confined to a wheelchair, likes to share her internet trouvailles with M'sieu Laurin . . .

"I just notice that on YouTube a 28-second sequence showing Asia Argento with the drool running off her long tongue has already got 40,613 clicks . . . right, and mine is the 40,614th . . . cute tongue, too."

Ed, in the background: "Signorina Argento is a twisted bourgeois. They all have tongues like that."

Anything
that Floats Your Boat, Padre

Alain has had one of his Dennis Lehane dreams (he admires the guy for "Mystic River" and a few other things): A drunk binge with Lansky has ended in the China Club, somewhere behind the Opéra Bastille, and now they are sitting outside the Eléphant du Nil near the St-Paul subway station on rue St. Antoine trying to piece together the events of the past three days.

A. apparently picked up a black teenage streetwalker in front of the Kube Hotel, in the 18th, where they spent a night . . .

LANSKY (61 years old, ruddy face, unruly salt-and-pepper hair, tall, somewhat out of shape): So what'd you do after?

A: I gave her cabfare.

LANSKY: She didn't use it.

A: She . . . what?

LANSKY: She came over to my room.

A: Your room. —(They stare at each other.)

A: So what you do after?

LANSKY: I rinsed my dick in the sink and drove her home.

A: You drove her home.

LANSKY: What. I'm speaking Czech?

A: People have a way of disappearing in your company. You drove her home.

LANSKY: I drove her home, yes.

A: Where'd she live?

LANSKY: Home.

*** (Gina: "I'm home, Will." —Will: "Let's kill him." Dennis Lehane, *Coronado*, 2005) ***

No, He Wears
a Ratty-Looking Balaclava

"There are no innocent bystanders. What were they doing there in the first place?" *William Burroughs*——The Sniper remembers things. His mind is a jumble of unrelated details, but the information is there, waiting to be used toward some disastrous end . . .

He remembers a guy with a rucksack running in a zigzag across the tarmac as a Boeing 757 is getting pulled away . . . He remembers Tegucigalpa after the hurricane. The city was an open sewer, buried in mud and bodies. Malaria broke out, and dengue fever. Rats carried leptospirosis, which causes liver and kidney failure and death. The smell of the rotting bodies was so thick you could taste it. There was this Chinese restaurant, half filled with mud and crushed furniture. All the food was spoiling and the sewers were overflowing and there were a lot of dirty diapers. They found the dead, crushed and twisted, under a platform. It was a low platform with tables and chairs on it, and the water had forced them under there . . .

On "Les Champs" a marcheuse (they are no longer allowed to stand in one place) follows him, quoting her price list ($200 —250 —300), then veers off, discouraged by his icy stare . . . He remembers getting blasted out of his sniper's nest in Côte d'Ivoire by a volley of mortar shells. And once again the space around him fills up with an abundance of incomprehensible objects and events . . . With his deactivated Taser he touches a fallen corpse, which immediately wriggles over and buries itself like a giant centipede in the earth . . .

He remembers an ormolu clock set to the wrong time ticking on his grandmother's mantel . . . He remembers a time when he was treated like a shitsmear on the sofa . . . He remembers putting out his Gitane in the jellied remains of a potato salad in a greasy spoon on rue Myrha and saying: "Sometimes, you aim for the centipede and hit the mushroom instead."——He remembers that she was not as attractive as she had appeared in the photograph. Perhaps it had been a trick of the nickeled Parisian light . . .

He remembers that a gram of coke in this flamenco club called Malasangre will set you back 60 Euro . . . He remembers his spotter, Tupelo Joe, lying in the red mud with half his face missing. A minute ago, Joe had been singing a Do-Wopper by the Coasters: "He wears a red bandana, Plays a cool pian-a . . . "

He remembers this: He shoots the guy down, stands over him. "You wearing Kevlar?" He pumps one in the guy's chest and answers his own question. "Yes. You know what I think? Kevlar is for twerps." He points the gun in the guy's face. "This is for Frank." BLAM . . .

And this: "The future of warfare is in the streets, highrise apartment buildings and sewers of failed cities the world over. Our recent military history is studded with names of cities such as Tuzla, Mogadishu, Los Angeles, Beirut, Saigon, Panama City, Port-au-Prince, Marseilles; yet those clashes are only the prologue to the drama awaiting us.'"(*Parameters*, Magazine of the Army War College, Spring 1996)

If he pulls it off, which is doubtful but possible, he may well become, in some countries, a cargo-cult figure. He is a mystery to them, but they know one thing—he is immortal. The Sniper is forever. He is, in fact, some kind of avenging hoodlum god who will hunt down and eliminate scum until the end of time.

Apparition on Boulevard Voltaire

At 2 AM, as he was about to get into a cab outside the Bataclan, he saw the black hooker from his latest Dennis Lehane dream crossing the street. He did a double-take, and for a second or two he felt so disoriented that he almost threw up.

Madame Blavatsky
Knew a Thing or Two

At Shakespeare & Co. he picks up a second-hand copy of Neil Gaiman's *Fragile Things* and opens it at random. To this: "I didn't know which one of the four was my dad, so I killed all of them. There were other men around St Andrew's who might have been my father, but after those four the joy went out of it."

He went outside and sat on the curb, next to two underage prostitutes in handcuffs. There are days when everything has a slimy pellucid significance.

The Egyptian

The room had the air of a Roman parlor gone to seed. The wood floor was rough for want of polish, the crown molding was nearly invisible beneath a dense layer of dust and grit. Two of the four walls were given over to bookshelves lined with a collection of works dealing with the history of the Middle East and Islam. The large mahogany desk was buried under piles of yellowed newspapers and a scattering of freshly opened mail. The room was in shadow, except for a shaft of sunlight which slanted through the half-open door.

The man behind the desk lowered the upper half of yesterday's Al-Ahram and fixed Alain in a lugubrious stare. He wore a wrinkled shirt of white Oxford cloth and a tan jacket with epaulettes. A lank forelock of gray hair fell toward a pair of dull bloodshot eyes. He scratched a carelessly shaved chin and lowered the volume on his radio. "You will be interested," he said in a petulant voice, "to hear my General Theory of Addiction in its entirety . . . "

Pet Sematary

"Here's a blog for you," he says to himself, staring at the screen in disbelief. "A vet in the Rocky Mountains, recording the animals she has to euthanize every day . . . 'June 13: A ferret with lymphoma, an adrenal tumor, and an insulinoma. She had no hair left and was covered in lymphatic lumps. She didn't look like a mammal anymore . . . June 14: An aged dachshund with cancer . . . A Pacman frog with a prolapsed ass . . . June 15: An old pet rat. He was just very old . . . Posted by WHAT-I-KILLED-TODAY at 11:40 PM. Comments: 0' "

L'Idée de l'Échec

He did not remember the faces of the women he had killed, but he knew the exact number and never stopped feeling their presence. They gave no indication that they were out to threaten and torture him; no, they seemed to think that he was an interesting guy to hang out with, so that on this evening, during dinner at Lansky's, they were once again sitting or standing around, some of them mouthing obscenities in his direction, others seemingly disinterested, pretending to busy themselves with adjusting an antimacassar or stepping in front of the maid as she served the mutton tajine.

The sickening inevitability of their deaths fouled up the air around him, and it was this pestilential aura which sometimes caused him to turn blue in the face and feel like he was suffering from the bends. He was, indeed, an intruder in an element clearly off-limits to him —a diver who should never again come up for air.

There had been a scorching hot day in July when he had thought that he had achieved it . . . toward midnight, on his back on some roof, looking up at the sky which underneath the sheen of the city's reflected lights still had that peculiar blue of deep oceans . . .

They Forget They're Dying

Officially, the Egyptian was making it as a clairvoyant. However, if you came with a recommendation he would also sell you a passport and a driver's license, the real thing, detoured by an Arab in the Meaux registration office, for 10 000 Euro.

He now shook an oval cigarette out of a pack open on his desk and lit up, inhaling hard. When he breathed out, there was no smoke: It had been soaked up by the spongy root and branch of his lungs. He flicked the pinkie of his left hand against a small cardboard container from some pharmaceutical company. "Gamma-Hydroxybutyrate," he said. "The date-rape drug. Works wonders for the terminally ill. They forget they're dying. Hope I can get some when it's my turn . . . "

Alain's thoughts wandered. He imagined going up to the attic, climbing out a garret-window and walking across the zinc-plated roofs, wet shirts and underwear flapping on a wire strung between two chimneys . . . And far away there will be other rooms, filled with the sort of light that glows from X-ray viewing screens . . . The walls are strangely displaced, as if a team of scene-shifters have pulled them back to create a new stage set . . . Sleepwalking, in the dead of night, he will find himself in Impasse Suez, below the Père Lachaise cemetery, and try to summon up the courage to pass through the wall . . . maybe with an offhand remark to a shadowy person to his left . . . "If it wasn't for the Wall of the Confederates I guess we'd be wading in the liquefied remains of Karl Marx's daughter now, I forget the name, Marie Laforgue . . . ?"

Get Your Fight Club Sunglasses Today ($175)

On Tuesday he spent an hour and a half in the Centre Pompidou. Standing in front of paintings and going into a kind of biostasis had a recreative effect on him. He liked paintings, even paintings he didn't understand. He bought art books sometimes and threw them out after a while. One of Julian Schnabel's plate paintings had prompted him to pose the question of the decade: Why force yourself to write a novel that has an idiotic plot when you can write a villanelle about waiting for the F Train?

For a fraction of a second he sees his right hand, glistening with fresh blood, as in a director's Shot Breakdown . . . "Fast

Pull-Out reveals hand (digital composite: stock + practical).” . . . Why is this popping up now. More of this to come? Will he at some point, at once frightened and fascinated, watch a movie called *The Story So Far*, revealing his lost years and the people x-ed out in his memory . . . Will they materialize before his eyes like the ghosts of escaped convicts who perished in a swamp . . .

We Deal in Lead

(Steve McQueen in *The Magnificent Seven*)——The sight picture disappeared in a blur of recoil. Yes, the rifle was held true; the scope, zeroed onto two hundred yards with a group size of less than two inches, was exactly where he wanted it; the trigger pull was smooth; he was surprised when it broke; his position was solid; no last second twitch, no flicker of doubt . . . So why the shivers? It worried him. He had never dreamed of a perfect shot and dived back into his body and felt his hands sliding across cold sweat on his stomach and chest . . .

His eyes shot open and he tasted salt and old copper pennies in his mouth and the windshield stretched and shivered in the instant before it shattered, showering him with a bucketful of glass, and the smell of dust and gasoline filled his nose and it took him a second or two to realize he was alive.

Haifa-sur-Seine

Atef Boukhrine did not disintegrate. But it certainly looked that way, and if you could have watched it in slow motion, you would have marveled at the Hollywood SFX quality of it; because the reddish cloud which in an instant replaced his neck blossomed into a crab nebula of blood mist and bone fragments and shredded skin and cartilage that made him look like a ninja doing a disappearing act.

He was the first of several suicide bombers that summer (anybody wearing a neck brace was now a clear and present danger) and he picked the Passage Jouffroy just as the Musée Grévin let out, with the result that his detonation wiped out half a busload of British tourists. "Haifa-sur-Seine" was the headline across the front page of Libération.

Alain Laurin, stepping into a McDonald's on Boulevard St. Germain, looked at images of the carnage on a wall-mounted TV and was having second thoughts about his sniper story.

Meanwhile, at the crime scene, the Commissaire of the Ninth had been shouldered aside by the Renseignements Généraux, while the RG encryption specialists were brooding over the surging internet chatter of Algerian 'sisters' . . . "merçi pr l'add c cool!! tu va bi1?.".. "jte kiffffffff ma soeur!!! à très vite nchallah . . . "

The Subway Mantra

The Sniper, in order to further his ability to concentrate on the job at hand, will at times recite one of his mantras —some of them rather silly, and all of them incomprehensible to anyone but him. There is a subway mantra he uses when he's riding the métro (right now he is on his way to Hôtel de Ville and his favorite breakfast place, Au Pain Quotidien in the rue des Archives) . . . "The F makes its last useful Manhattan stop at West Fourth. You get off, switch to the A. The A stops at Chambers, same as the E, but the E goes much deeper into the station, all the way to the World Trade Center. You switch to the A, you save about a half-mile of walking if it's Chambers you really want."

He knows that his days as a pro are a distant memory, and he is now just a Sloppy Joe with a gun —although not as sloppy as Breton ("The surrealist act par excellence is to rush out into the street and start blasting away.") In any case, he expects to kill approximately a hundred people. And in an increasingly erratic way: In the early stages he will at some point do two arrondissements on the same day, and not adjoining ones either. And on the first three days he will be firing his rounds protected by the noise of jackhammers etc. (After that, he assumes, they will catch on and close down all construction work in the city). He may even do an additional hit, outside the arrondissements, perhaps in Passy, with a 12-gauge Rossi from one of the villas there, confusing those who think he'll be too proud to use a shotgun . . .

Les Disparues de Calais

The Erinnyas of Alain Laurin aka GL23 are taking a break from shadowing his activities, and from the heat which hovers around 110 degrees and slows life in the city to a weary insect crawl. Time jumps as they board the night ferry to Folkestone in a series of jerky out-of-focus shots that make them look like anatomically challenged creatures from outer space.

They pause to admire the woolworthian chutzpah of the souvenir shop. One — is it the Jane Doe from San Francisco Bay? — is mesmerized by a T-shirt that says SAVE A DRUM, BANG A DRUMMER. Then they are all sitting around the large table in the center of the fish 'n' chips and sandwich place. There is food in front of them, but they can't get interested. What's the point if you are dead.

Kick Out the Jams for the Passacaglia

Elvira Lansky has a live-in Filipino driver/wheelchair-pusher called Joe (for "Joselito," she says) who once a month, on a late Sunday afternoon, delivers her to some strangely impoverished nondescript Armenian church or other for a concert of late 17th century Italian muzak; so today Alain decides to tag along —to St. Ephrem's, near the Panthéon —and case the joint, as it were.

Sure enough, Saint Eph turns out to be a perfect location for the Sniper: The rifle will be taped to one of the organ pipes way in the back of the instrument, and he can shoot at people from the squat tower as they are leaving after a service, with the droning sounds of the organ filling the church so that only those outside can hear the shots - and get hit half a second later; and the Sniper can then come down and mingle with the crowd. He would. He's the type. Cold-blooded bastard. Antifreeze running in his veins . . . On the other hand, A. reminds himself—don't get too fancy. Murphy's Law, all that . . .

"Paris Nous Appartient" (J. Rivette). Wrong.

"Perhaps," he reflects the following morning on quai Montebello, "Madame likes to listen to scratchy third-string fiddlers because they deserve no pity. Naturally, The Sniper would gladly alert you to the fact that anyone willing to listen to that crap deserves to die . . . " He is looking at Gucci handbags from China, Rolex watches draped inside trenchcoats, necklaces large as wind chimes, digital cuckoo clocks and curling tongs from Korea. A mint copy of *Dialéctica y canibalismo* by Alberto Cardin, Editorial Anagrama, Barcelona 1994. And a throaty scream on the front page of yesterday's Sunday Telegraph: "Jail guard sent me pervy texts!"

He fondly remembers Joselito saying, about a former employer: "Once you're saddled with a colostomy bag, you'll always feel uncomfortable no matter what you're wearing, there's always this Thing, comprende, it slaps against your right thigh, it gurgles and gargles at your lower back . . . Believe me, refusing to turn into a total cynic is a full-time job. 'And for God's sake don't have an accident! I don't want to die in these clothes!' . . . "

Good old Joe, in his early fifties, an avid reader of mangas, and he's got a mum on Mindanao who collects roadkill and keeps it in her freezer. According to Elvira, he's a big hit with the whores of rue St. Denis . . . Hard to believe if you look at him: Bushy eyebrows, empty scalp, John Lennon glasses, a hanging shoulder . . . you'd think a public library employee caught in a pedophile sweep . . .

Alain feels that he should perhaps share this with Mrs. Lansky.

"Ed's not here," she says.

"El . . . does it ever occur to you that . . . "

". . . you might want to talk to ME? Come on. Nobody wants to talk to a cripple."

"Yes, ma'm. Where's Ed?"

"In Scotland, talking to A.L. Kennedy. And both of them enjoying the lousy weather. Probably tying one on, too. She's said to be a fearsome lush. And now for something completely different: I got my armpits shpritzed with Botox, spare me the splotched T-shirt for six months, minimum. No more sweat running from ze creux de l'aisselle. You are welcome to use my nurse. She'll do it for a sawski."

Towards a
Unified Field Theory of Ghosts

A unified field theory of ghosts should answer, for starters, some of the more elementary questions that keep getting in the way, and it should do so utilizing a pragmatic approach à la *Ghostbusters*. So . . .

Why don't they fly to Cornwall and its cool air and brac- ing breeze from the Atlantic Ocean on broomsticks or by stretching the right arm with the index finger extended? Because on the night ferry from Calais, in the company of people puking over the rail, they can feel a little less insub- stantial. It's like a contact high in the company of junkies.

Why do they have to flee the shvitz and swelter of August in Paris in the first place? Because the air is getting uncom- fortably dense around them; they feel a friction and find it difficult to move around. It's something to do with the humidity really; or atmospheric moisture, whatever.

And why do they need to get in a huddle in front of the TV screen? (Alain can't help sensing their presence whenever the TV image gets a little fuzzy . . .) Well, they don't see so good. They are, like, near-sighted. Their sight can be com- pared to that of a weak infrared camera. They want to see something, they have to get close. They also have to know when to stop getting close, or they'll pass right through it . . .

Fais Gaffe, Nenette

Why would the Sniper pick on Passy? Maybe he made a note of it when he saw *Ultimo Tango*, with Brando under the bridge there doing his Eniwetok Paulie routine ... "Fuck God in the face! Fuck Mom and her rancid cunt cobwebbed with disuse! Fuck her apple pie, and fuck the dog that's been humping her under the magnolia tree! Shit!"

And in front of the TV cameras he gives them his goofy grin and says: "Let's just say we're taking a flying fuck on a rolling donut ... " And Bertolucci falls to his knees and whimpers "I'm-a not worthy to do his shoelaces. E vero!" And at the Actors Studio they are committing mass harakiri. And to round it out let's have a shmaltzy little Musette waltz in the background: "Ah, pauv' Nenette ... j'vas t'casser la gueule sous le Pont de Passy, espèce de tantouze récyclée ... "

On a more serious note, A. has been keeping a logbook listing all the spots and places he can no longer go near without squirming in the clutches of full-tilt angst and feeling his blood pressure skyrocket. The result is that Paris, for him, is seriously shrinking: A single toxic spot can contaminate an entire quartier. This will be difficult to handle ... 20 rue du Sénégal, below the Parc de Belleville ... the blue door of the Club St. Germain (long closed and abandoned) ... the Hôtel Mondial near Place de la République ... The mysterious Père Lachaise grave of Lee Miller (it is empty —her ashes were scattered on her farm in Sussex). There are even two subway stations with irritating names that sound like stops in Cape Town: Buzenval, Exelmans ...

A Phantom Voice from 1860 Paris

(Right. It's a drunk singing "Don't fence me in . . . " recorded on a strip of paper covered with soot by a French inventor
who tried to beat *la mère* Alva Edison by a year or two.)

Alain had read up on Lee Miller a day after he had sat on the
polished granite slab covering her empty grave and suffered
a mild stroke that scared him shitless. She had been sexually
abused by her father when she was a child; on photographs
taken by the perp she looks like an hypnotically beautiful
alien. It's her eyes, which are radiant and empty at the same
time. They are gray-green and appear to be translucent.

She was Man Ray's girlfriend and model for two years,
around 1931/32, and his most famous and disturbing painting is of her lips hovering like a giant spaceship above a
desolate landscape with an observatory.

In August 1944, a war photographer for *Vogue*, she was one of
the first into Paris (with a canary in a cage to warn them of
poison gas —by dropping dead. They called him Die Hard
2) —and the first American to come up the spiral staircase
to Picasso's studio on the Left Bank, with a bottle of bub-
bly and a hearty "How they hangin', Pablo?" A few weeks
later she photographed herself sitting in Hitler's bathtub
in Munich and using his loofah.

The day, and the strange place, of the stroke is actually a
less polluted memory than some of those other spots . . . .
and he will record more of them like he's taking dictation
from a nasty succubus.

Asking for It in the Boondocks

"We'll kill 'em all." (Saudi terrorist grandpa, most of his fingers missing, in "Operation Kingdom")

They are having breakfast outside the Café Charbon on rue Oberkampf, a former coal and firewood place. For Elvira this amounts to slumming.

"You notice," she says, "that M'sieu le Président, in order to get a dozen presumed guilty ones arrested in the projects, has to send a thousand police, riot police, SWAT teams, what-have-you. Plus firefighters and several EMS trucks. A thousand."

Alain seems to remember something. "Wasn't it a thousand beurs from the suburbs who attacked that protest march of college students last year with iron bars and bicycle chains?"

"That's right. Planned like a military operation."

"I guess it means that the two sides are now communicating at batallion strength."

Joselito lights a cheroot and says with a laugh: "The hombre in the Matignon keeps saying: It's a police problem. It will be a police solution."

"Bullshit," says Mrs. Lansky. "I talk to my acquaintances in the uh services, and the general feeling is that we have a state of siege. 'There's five million of them out there!' That's the theme song in the white population. It will be a military solution, you ask them. As soon as there is another riot in

Courneuve or some other ghetto, they'll bring in a brigade of paratroopers from Clermont-Ferrand."

"Urban warfare," says Alain. "Where have I heard that before."

Choking Game
Claims 82 Young Lives in US

Brigitte, 13, is the daughter of Henri Mayat, the Louisiane's manager. "I'm being . . . what's the word . . . ostracized," she says, sprawled Lolita-like on the divan next to the potted yucca. "Love that word. Ostracized. In school and out."

Alain raises an eyebrow. "How come?"

"Because I refuse to go to parties anymore."

"And why is that?"

"Cause the minute you walk in, the guys are practically ordering you to give head. I'm sick and tired of this shit. The Kalahari niggers have more sense, and a better attitude."

"How d'you know?"

"I've been there."

"Oh."

"And 78% of the guys enjoying a higher education in this country want to be civil servants."

"Says who."

"National Office of Statistics. Isn't that fuckin' hilarious?"

She then reports that, with the help of the boys on the mezzanine, she plans to hack into the Lycée Voltaire computer and alter —with extreme prejudice —the recent grades of certain male evildoers.

A Braille Dildo for Your G-Spot, Jean

Cocteau, as a kid, on his way home from school used to run his fingertips through the grooves in a stone wall near his parents' house, humming his private songlines and in effect recording them in stone. Decades later, he says (in *Opium*), he still could feel his way through the old stories with his fingertips. He's probably lying. But as an idea it isn't half bad.

For A. it doesn't work that way. His past is a landscape pockmarked with ugly patches of quicksand where he caused, or suffered, degradation and defeat, and the blighted terrain stays with him and is getting difficult to negotiate. There are days when he wishes he could look back with the equanimity of Morris Lefkowitz, the gangster: "I seen a lot of bad shit in my time, and I'm still eating lox."

They're into Trees Now

"I think dying is a very hard business, however achieved." Martha Gellhorn, war reporter and suicide. Those were the days.

The fundamentalist insurgents' camp is in a former ninja/paintball amusement park in a forest near Chevreuse. The BB cops (brigade anti-banditisme or something) had an undercover agent in there who has since disappeared. The entire forest is owned, indirectly, by the Muslim Brotherhood which gets part of its funding from Saudi Arabia.

The Brothers have established, under the cover of some Union of Islamic Organizations, a bridge-head in the most depressing part of La Courneuve, north of Paris, in a drab squat building surrounded by garbage, broken furniture and car wrecks. The building's ground floor is a large prayer hall with industrial carpeting and a lot of fire extinguishers.

The garbage out there flared up again just the other day when a 15-year-old beur, in order to defend his family's honor, doused his sister with gasoline and put a match to her because she allowed a classmate to buy her an ice-cream and accompany her to the bus stop. It does not occur to the bearded ones to clear the combustible detritus away. It would be like telling them to eat breaded pig snout.

Laughter of the Dead

(Cioran would have loved this): Most of the laugh tracks on television were recorded in the early 1950s. These days, most of the people you hear laughing are dead.

"Describe," reads the latest entry in Alain Laurin's notebook, "after a final look at the dead bodies, the abandoned city, like a curdled amoeba seen from the air." He is going to shoot for the one event that will make the Sniper obsolete forever: The detonation of a dirty bomb on Place de la Concorde.

Daylight leaking over the rooftops . . . a Dept. of Sanitation truck with spinning brushes is polishing the curbs, spraying them with water that seems to evaporate in seconds . . . a hint of dew is glistening briefly on the metal shutters of shops closed for the rest of the month . . . one of the scandal sheets is lamenting the fact that a gingko tree planted by Marie-Antoinette is dying for lack of water . . . "You'd think somebody would empty a pail of dishwater around the damn thing, but no! Let it croak! What the hell!".. the flattened carcasses of two dogs that got run over by APCs are shoveled into green plastic bin liners . . . there are very few people on the streets; they are carrying big bottles of Evian and Vittel, splashing water over their heads every hundred yards or so . . . a detail of German soldiers is leaving the Senate building on this 4th of August, 1944, marching down the boulevard . . . the submachine guns slung over their shoulders are held horizontally, in firing position . . . suddenly, they break formation and start spraying the people on the sidewalks with bursts of exactly .8 seconds.

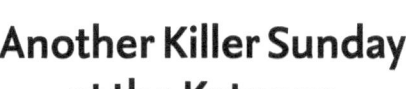

Another Killer Sunday at the Katanga

The Katanga is the only place in the neighborhood that is open for business on Sunday mornings. It has a zinc-topped counter with black olives and hard-boiled eggs in glass bowls and pieces of bruschetta con pesto on a chipped plate. There is a blackboard menu above two barrels of port and an ancient nickeled cash register that catches the light and does an ugly BLINGG–CLANGG when it is opened and banged shut.

Alain is standing at the counter writing in his notebook, and he is writing in the first person plural because he senses that his harem of lost souls, back from Cornwall, is once again following him around . . .

"The place smells of coffee and grilled cheese, and you want to hug La Mère Wilsdorff, bless his mercenary soul, for taking the edge off these rotten Sundays when Paris is at its worst. We order sliced meats, bread and cheese, black coffee, a glass of sherry. We have squishy armpits, and our shirts are clinging to our backs and salty sweat is running down everybody's face. The lone ceiling fan stirring the stale hot air is only something to look at, the ice cube machine has conked out, it is 38 degrees Celsius, and the heat doesn't let up at night, and yet you are looking into happy faces, and Souad Massi is singing 'Talit el bir.' . . . Lansky has sent his people off to the Atlantic coast: 'Jump in the ocean and come out with goosebumps and blue lips and eventually you'll feel a craving for your heat-soaked office and something useful to do . . .' He is doing a bad job of staying behind and pretending to run his outfit 'under ideal conditions, all by myself . . .' The breakfast room at the hotel this morning stank of used condoms and rancid Nivea AfterSun, and the Krauts were playing, with hysterical abandon, a card game they call Sh-kaht . . . Why not kill some of those East German proles for a change."

Walk Like an Egyptian

About 200 yards up the street from the Café Charbon you reach the Cour Mauresque, a dead-end alley behind a porte cochère just wide enough to allow delivery trucks. It is an idyllic place with patches of amaryllis and dysentery-colored dahlias in front of old-style print shops and picture-framers and design studios. An old woman with a mop and bucket is swabbing the ancient cobble stones worn smooth by countless feet and handcarts loaded with potatoes, briquettes and corn cobs.

The Cour M widens at the end, and on the right, behind a trellis overgrown with bougainvillea, there is a grungy old gym, mostly used by weather-beaten characters in sleeveless vests whose veins pop out of their heads when they are on the bench press. On the opposite side of the turnaround, in a former bicycle repair shop, an old Syrian cabinetmaker and his three sons are fixing old furniture, while in the back room — brought in each day and picked up again by two Citroen vans that look like Nissen huts on wheels — a bunch of zealots are conditioning the wives of a dozen fallen freedom-fighters toward a major terrorist torch event in a world-famous public space . . . And it is at the entrance to Cour M that Alain one morning spots the Egyptian who has not been seen since the day of Atef Boukhrine's suicide mission.

Courtney Love Chased by Werewolf in Benedict Canyon

On this night, the Harem of Lost Souls congregated around a pauper's grave in Clairvaux (Burgundy), within sight of the jail where the inhabitant of the hole in the ground had done sixteen years of hard time. It was the exact time of day when, ten years ago, Gerald Lake's deviant mother had died in her cell, with some of the ghosts present jumping up and down on her chest. She probably would have died anyway, but they liked to think that they had contributed to her demise —they had trampled around on her numerous times before, and each time she had jolted upright on her bunk and screamed in abject terror.

Clairvaux had been founded by a monk named Bernard who later became famous. On June 25, 1115, accompanied by a dozen followers, he arrived in Absinth Valley, as it was then called, and started work on a monastery. And then became the founder of fifty more, as well as a kind of 12th century Catholic bin Laden: He preached the Second Crusade which turned into a total flop and cost seven million lives.

"I guess she somehow intuits who we are and is giving us a wide berth, is why we never collide with her," says the vic from Avenue C in Manhattan.

"She intuits nothing," says another. "She was a nut then, and she's remained one."

"The Est Républicain called her La Folle de Troyes."

"Yeah, but the court determined that she was fully responsible."

"He could have killed her, instead of us."

"Not according to Freud."

"Oh sure . . . " Exaggerated yawns all around.

In recent years they have made it a habit to check up on Carlos the Jackal in his Spartan cell devoid of any extras. They melt through the southeast wall. He is snoring on his bunk. There is a soggy sock on the cement floor. Apparently he managed to jack off before falling asleep.

"For a womanizing terrorist he sure looks shitty," says the ex-driver of the black Subaru.

Avenue C takes a look at the papers on his small desk. "Look, he's changed his name again . . . to, hm, Idries Süleiman . . . and now he's writing for a militant rag 'published at a secret location in eastern Turkey' . . . "

A Jane Doe named Lucy sits on the inmate's abdomen and assumes the position of Rodin's thinker. "I jump up and down on the old cunt's stomach and I don't even feel winded," she reminisces morosely. "What a waste of . . . something."

"Wouldn't it be nice," says Ave. C, "to shop for ramen and frozen mollusk in the Stuyvesant Place Sunrise Mart above the St. Mark's Bookshop on The Bowery. It's a hunnerd percent Jap now . . . then slurp a bowl of hot udon at Soba-ya on Ninth . . . "

"Will you shut up, goddammit! How long does it take you to grasp that your time as an eater . . . is toast! So to speak . . ." That cracks everybody up. Their mute laughter is a gruesome sight.

I Paid for Pain
(www.sltattoostudio.com)

In the early days of his criminal career, a vice cop had offered to sell him a snuff movie, calling the flick "diseased." Interesting choice of word. For a sales pitch. It had been a female cop. Who didn't have a clue as to how . . . close she came.

If asked to characterize his existence, he probably would use words like crippled and redundant rather than depraved and yucky. The morally correct adverb is never accurate.

He finds it endlessly fascinating to listen to Elvira Lansky making statements of zen-like unsentimentality: "I've made a will. I want my ashes sprinkled off the end of Margate Pier." And to watch the effect it has on her husband: A brief, soulful glance in her direction . . . Apparently it is easier, and more rewarding, to love somebody who is hopelessly ill.

"Well," says Lansky, solidly in his cups, "in the next life we'll demand better cell phones and better coke in ritzier toilets ... "

"I forgot to ask," says Alain, " —did you bag AL Kennedy?"

"She's an interesting writer who can't be had. I'll do Norma Rivington instead."

"And Norma ... "

" ... is the former head of MI5."

"Turned pulp writer."

"C'est ça."

"Welcome to the club, ma'm. Don't park on the lawn."

Dream of the Long Island Jewish

On the steps leading to the maternity ward he remembers the medical district in some southern city, six hospitals in a seven-block area, connected by breeze ways and parking lots, a food court in the center of the tallest building so the anxious and the grieving and the doctors and the bedpan cleaners can eat, Sbarro, Au Bon Pain, Panda Express, Dunkin' Donuts ... had he been there on business? In any case, he has been about to stab a pregnant blonde in the parking lot when a feeling of total desolation and hopelessness stopped him in his tracks ... and while he is sitting on the steps there waiting to see if another one will trigger the . . . the . . . whatever it is that drives him to do it . . . a prowl car stops at the foot of the stairs and the cops are trying to drag an elderly pregnant woman from the back seat . . . and as she is fighting them, screaming and clawing, her voice is giving her away, and he realizes it's his mother, or a close approximation . . . he turns away and fights an urge to barf all over the place . . .

"Sit back and enjoy the mayhem," says an orderly wearing a hassidic Panama hat made of silky black moleskin. His frock, sprayed with chemicals to mask the smell of other chemicals, is flapping in the wind. Alain, or is it his other self, tries to convince himself that he's turned in a flawless performance so far, professional, not a second of indecision . . . I have never stalked a woman, and I will not start today . . . I see her, I kill her. End of story. Don't want to know how dull their job is, how far they are along, how big their house; or look at photographs of their children who have names that sound like brands of shampoo. Meet Nivea Saunders. Diesel Dyke van Dyke. And here's a Native American, former child prodigy on the bandoneon: Joey Umbrella Corporation. Shantih, everybody. Paakhi . . . Bengali for bird. What's in a name. Pfffhh.——A patient on a trolley. Looks like a fat fly caught in a web of tubes and wires. The skin around her mouth is puckered and dry. The monitor flatlines. Orderlies hopping up and down in frustration.

"I drove all night," says Roy Orbison from a transistor radio, "and lemme tell you —the exposed socks look isn't gonna fly in Hollywood because that's where we keep our weed . . . " Did he say weed? Pretentious nance . . . hey, I just laughed

my drink into my lungs . . . hyrch! . . . aw, gimme a break . . .
this is so diseased . . .

The Rhizome Writers Initiative
Is Supported by PERNOD

Youp! Zoust! Ca cogne infect! (L-F Céline)——He likes to
be up and about at daybreak, on account of the fucken heat,
and besides, it is always 4 a.m. in the multi-user dungeon
of the Soul.

This morning he is walking across Place de la Concorde,
looking up at the obelisk which Napoleon stole from Egypt
and on top of which the dirty bomb will be detonated by
the arrant believers. It'll be the revenge of Isis, Anubis, Idi
Amun, Idries Suleyman, you name 'em. Making Paris un-
inhabitable at the snap of a finger.

Two hundred years from now, gothic pirate scum, mutated
beyond the pale, will do a cannibal shindig on the exact spot
where the guillotine decapitated the king . . . And the tattered ghosts of rescue divers from Petit Clamart will search,
one final futile time, for the drowned bodies of Isadora
Duncan's kids downstream from the Ile de Puteaux . . . The
two children rolled into the Seine on the backseat of her
Bugatti when the chauffeur went for a pack of cigarettes and
forgot to pull the handbrake. Son cosas de la vida.

And the umpteenth clone of Mireille Mathieu, completely
unrecognizable now, will stand on a small stage in a former

Dixieland cave in Rue de la Huchette, surrounded by a bevy of teenage existentialists in black leotards and turtleneck sweaters, and she'll sing in a brittle alto: "Just cover your head when you're dead . . . and take out the garbage and fuck me, Fred . . . aw mama can this really be the end . . . here's that mummy with the Memphis Blues again . . . it's really ENDLESS!!! . . . "

A High Wind in Waziristan

Norma Rivington's book is available at Brentano's. It describes two Paki terrorists producing C4 bombs in the English countryside. The description is detailed, but slightly off. Probably meant to entice dumb ragheads to give it a try and have the product blow up in their faces. Unless they manage to displease their employers before they get to the tricky part. In which case they will wash up on the mudflats off Foulness Island. The dogfish have had a go at their noses and cheeks, and they have to be identified by their teeth.

The two Salaafist fanatics in their basement bomb factory on Rue Myrha, in the Eighteenth, have done a crash course in Waziristan, at the end of which the instructor sang out over the barren landscape: "Composition Four . . . The north, south, east and west winds of Jihad! Al-hamdou-lillah!"

They are model believers who will interrupt the good work five times a day to roll out the prayer rug and prostrate themselves in the general direction of Mecca. On the day of Ashura, in February, they could be seen in a backyard mosque in Goutte d'Or lashing their backs with braided leather whips. In any case . . . when working with unstable mixtures you do not interrupt the job for your prayer duties. It's a stupid thing to do, and the Prophet does not approve of it.

In the makeshift basement kitchen the two Algerians rolled up their sleeves. They knew the routine —the urban warfare cadre had been made to memorize it back at the camp. Boil the water . . . add two packs of clear gelatin . . . mix it in . . . let it cool for a couple of minutes . . . add half a cup of cooking oil . . . stir . . . a thin surface crust of solids will begin to form . . . skim them off with a spoon, and in a Tupperware box put them in the freezer compartment of the refrigerator . . .

The Midnight Rambler

A tall Sahaouri wearing a deep blue turban and an ankle-length burnous of the same color got off the 5 train on the lowest platform underneath Place de la République shortly before midnight.

Alain, along with three other passengers getting out of the same car, started to follow the tall one to the blue sign that said "Sortie." Within seconds, they all noticed that the man was having trouble adjusting the right strap of his Jack Wolfskin rucksack which appeared to be weighed down by something at once heavy and delicate . . .

As upon an invisible sign, they turned around and at a brisk pace made for the other exit at the far end of the platform.

Remembrance of Things Past

To get rid of the traffic noise from the boulevard, A. relocated to a room on the top floor going on the narrow inner court of the Louisiane. A Portuguese cleaning-woman told him that a former occupant of Room 79 had jumped out of the window on the left. The guy's ghost was probably at that very moment standing on the horizontal part of the zinc roof over there, eyeing him quizzically.

If you leaned out over the window's iron bar, the perpendicular view was hugely depressing alright. Alain decided that what prevented him from following the suicide's trajectory was the bottle of 2003 Montepulciano d'Abruzzo, still three-quarter full, on the small refrigerator next to the writing desk.

In the morning an ancient gent in a faded mustard green suit had been talking to the receptionist—face like a hatchet, ears like someone left the car doors open; looked like a worthy successor to the late Albert Cossery. The hotel still attracted a good mix: Those who wanted to die, and those who refused to die.

On days when he cannot write he often sits in a corner of his room for hours, rattling off recollections, circling the forgotten years —maybe, he thinks, if he keeps it up he will eventually penetrate the "membrane" and find access to the inner circle of Paddy O'Blivion, as he calls it; like a spy getting next to the Brotherhood bridge-head managers in Courneuve . . . most of them maimed or crippled or incomplete. Some of them are said to have faces like melted plastic. It's a damaged life, theirs and his, and he expects to find more of the same.

He remembers endless night drives, as a courier for a successful team of B&E specialists on the Côte d'Azur, to Perpignan and Barcelona, obsessed with the idea that it should be possible to scat along with the bass solos of Scott LaFaro and Gary Peacock when they had been part of the Bill Evans trio in the early sixties. It was clearly impossible to match them note for note, but after several months, and with the tape cassette nearly worn out, he had gotten close.

He remembers the day he burst into hysterical laughter when he heard Edward Norton say, in *Fight Club:* "I'm free. Losing all hope means freedom." He had tried to segue into a hacking cough, but they had insisted that he leave the theater.

At some point, out of curiosity, he had paid serious money to watch an almost-celebrity couple fuck and have fun in a villa near Florence. He had decided against it within two or three minutes, because it dawned on him that the fun aspect of any fuck could only get twisted and contaminated by the fact that it was observed by a creature like him.

Which reminded him of a diary entry in a pictorial biography of Theodore W. Adorno: The smallish plump Kraut philosopher, during his exile in New York City, had whipped a prostitute into unconsciousness —and the next morning, he claimed, both of them woke as "improved human beings." What a sick hick. "W" stands for Wiesengrund which is not really translatable, but A. likes to think of the guy as "Deep Lawn." ———

112 degrees in the shade, and Ben Vautier gets to design the front page of "Charlie Hebdo"——"Suez! Bande de ratés!" (Sweat! Gaggle of losers.)

"So, Hey, You Guys Are Werewolves, Too … Cool …"

(*American Werewolf in Paris*, 1987)——Joselito at the Haynes, in the Ninth, a funky hang-out established by a black ex-G.I. in 1947. Joe loves to start breakfast by doing a grotesque pinched-face rendition of his Brit employers' mannerisms (he's had several): "Cuppa broken peacock Assam, slice of Hollywood Diet Bread, nub end of Cheddar, just this side of edible … The trouble with big breakfasts, they make you hungry for the rest of the day." He laughs uproariously. In front of him there's a stack of pancakes glistening with maple syrup and melted butter, and for seconds he has ordered shrimp gumbo.

"Remember the basketball court in the Champ de Mars park? With a full view of the Eiffel Tower? It's been taken over by beurs. Used to be BNP trainees, students, so forth. Not anymore. Now it's Maghreb toughs. Big guys. Black belt types. They're not good at basketball. Just pretending. And denying the court to anyone else. For hours. In the evening the *gardien* comes along and orders them off the court. They say 'Sure …' —and climb up the chainlink fence. Sit there like Hitchcock's birds. Glaring at him. He locks the gate, moves on. They climb down, start to party, with a ghetto-blaster and plenty of hooch. Nobody bothers them. A statement of some sort, I guess … "

"Drearily predictable, too. It says: 'You'll need a hundred CRS to get us out of here.'"

Deep-Sixed in Thiais

"The noon heat raised sour smells from the milk in dumped lattes in trash cans and gutters. Second-story air conditioners dripped condensation like fat raindrops." Lee Child, *The Hard Way.*

Le Point reported 15,000 dead so far, mostly elderly people, victims of the hottest summer in a hundred years, in Paris alone. The mayor claimed it was only 2800. He offered no explanation for the fact that gravediggers were working punishing shifts, 24/7, and had already buried some of their own. There was talk of mass graves with layers of 50-100 bodies covered with quicklime.

Noureddine Boudjenah, the team leader, took three pipe cleaners, pushed them through the slowly cooling wax of the central sphere and out the other side —and twisted the ends together for connection to the detonator hook-ups. The triple-cascade C4 detonation had always been favored by the Salaafist groups operating in France. It was, you might say, their signature; and he was about to sign off.

"I don't know if you have seen this," says Lansky waving a handful of newsprint. He is sweating profusely in his deserted publishing office. The fans are off because he hates to have pages flying through the air. "The Guardian calls your latest effort 'sensationally nasty' . . . "

Alain is touched. "That is high praise indeed. I guess I prefer it over 'girdle-busting escapism'."

Lansky is horrified. "No! Tell me you're making this up . . . "

" 'Fraid not. Women's Wear Daily."

"The deeply devious . . . dipshit twats! . . . "

Alain nods. "May they fall down and be paralyzed."

None of Them Knew
They Were Robots

There, among all the remembered detritus, is a video clip of JG Ballard in his Pontiac, circa 1971, stating with a straight face: "The multi-storey car park is one of the most mysterious structures ever built."

There is spooky Vashti Bunyan somehow still looking like she did thirty-five years ago when she played her fiddle surrounded by slippery rocks and the airborne foam of the Irish Sea.

There is a pestilential hole in the ground, and if you close your eyes and dive into the muck you come out the other end and it's another pestilential hole in the ground.

There is the make-believe hip email from the Algerian "sister" to the Crazy Horse dancer she is trying to convert to The Cause (and both of them on the radar of DNAT —Division Nationale Anti-Terroriste): "J'kiff comment tu parles . . . T'iras loin, Incha'Allah."

'A long time they remained almost motionless, like certain insects you see mating.' (Simenon, *The Bells of Bicêtre*) Don't you wish you were an insect sometimes, the dancer writes in her Poesie-Album (she's ex-GermanDemocraticRepublic). Just freeze. Hibernate. Get your dick shredded in the suction hole of a vacuum cleaner.

The Egyptian has soaked through the cracks of the world and vanished. His name was Abd El-Sayeed Basouni, and he looked like an ad for dendrophilia ("sex with trees" as one of his shadowers helpfully added in his report to the section chief).

The DNAT section chief has to tell his superiors that his people have lost all trace of their man. The mugwumps bust him to the equivalent of lavatory attendant.

His replacement was an old hand on loan from the DST Middle East unit who had been stationed in Larnaka, Cyprus. This one had a visceral distrust of his colleagues in the various branches of the French security system. It wasn't the terrorists, the spies and the other dangers to national security you had to worry about, it was the bastard in the next office who would be happy to stab you in the back.

He has recommended himself with a lengthy paper on the subject of "What makes a cheap YouTube clip go viral?" His conclusion —it must be brief, controversial and good lethal fun. Such as the recently posted clip on the Body Farm in Tennessee. Or that Mexican sculptress, what's her name, who had an installation of mummies in a Frankfurt museum where visitors got sprayed with body fluid from corpses.

"Make me a video," he says to his technical people, "of how we dig up the guy's dead mother in Aswan and dump her on the black rock in Mecca from a helicopter. We'll smoke out that feelthy Egyptian wherever he may be."

His knowledge is encyclopedic. He is not easily fooled. He can even tell you that the Caveau de la Huchette, a dixieland tourist trap, used to be a torture chamber during the Revolution.

Skip to My Loo

The 19-year-old Japanese student in a bistro near the Conservatoire had a large foldout page of sheet music on her table. She told Alain that it was a piece for piano, didgeridoo and Japanese one-string fiddle which looks and is played like a skinny cello. The concert grand was to be used exclusively as a percussion instrument.

The notations on the page looked like cut-up hexagrams of the I Ching. She demonstrated five bars' worth of rhythmic figures the percussionist would have to produce, tapping them out with the fingers of both hands as well as her left foot, and sang hiccupy lines of the didgeridoo that went against and between all of the others. The complexity was vertiginous.

"The one-string has the easy part," she explained. "He or she simply does a funky Hokkaido hoedown."

The Sniper casually slashed the rainproof cloth top, dipped in his hand, slipped the lock and slid into the driver's seat. He smashed his right heel into the covering below the steering column. It was plastic, but old plastic, and half of it cracked away, revealing the white metal ignition barrel beneath.

He yanked the four wires out and stripped them back with the knife. Taking the red main ignition lead he quickly touched it to the other wires in turn. With the third, a green wire, there was a brief lurch as the starter turned over.

Isolating the green wire, he connected the other two to the red one. The dashboard was now live. Depressing the clutch, he ran through the gears a couple of times and forced himself to breathe evenly.

Avoiding the electric shocks he'd suffered earlier outside the Flèche d'Or in Belleville, he touched the green starter wire to the other three and tipped the accelerator, and the motor howled. He put the car in reverse, let off the handbrake and backed out of the parking space down the block from the Kube Hotel.

Even the gentlest push of the big toe seemed to get a deep snarl from the old sports car. The Sniper nodded, shifted to first and drove off. He had just stolen the vintage '64 magenta Triumph TR4 (red leather seats, new top) of Edward Lansky, publisher.

Unlike the Elephant Man, the men with faces like melted plastic and transplanted penis cartilage will not cover up. They are, like the FAHP commandos, walking nightmares, and they have begun to flaunt it. Theirs is the more powerful narrative, and they intend to deliver it with the inevitability of a heat-seeking missile.

No Soy Como Era Antes

"L'homme vulnérable doit éviter tout éclat." (Talleyrand) Never was a truism so true. Getting screwed by a brazen garcon at the Café de Flore and having to take it sitting down because you can't afford to draw attention to yourself . . . A. just hates it. However, he is surrounded by five of the Erinnyas who are presently swinging into their classic Greek tragedy chorus routine, soundlessly hissing into both of the culprit's ears at once.

"I don't believe this!"

"Cheating our guy out of forty cents!"

"Not only are you a thieving scumbag, you are a CHEAP scumbag!"

"Get me the manager! On the double!"

"I want to see your sorry ass in the gutter! Right here!"

"You know what you are? You're a waterbug on the toilet seat, that's what you are!"

The waiter hesitates. Next, he seems to reel. Not much, but . . . perceptibly.

Alain gets up, leaving a Euro and a half on the table. And says, almost touching the waiter's nose with his own: "That's what you should have tried to cheat me out of. If you had the guts."

He turns on a customer who makes as if to remonstrate with him. He is doing the hissing now. "Get this: I'm not a fuckin' Austrian! I can afford to tell this tosser off all I want! Freely!"

In the Grand Palais he stopped in front of a large canvas painted after a news photo of 1968 or '69 showing a captured B-52 pilot named Robinson, hands tied behind his back, on a path between endless rice paddies in North Vietnam. And next to him an NVA girl soldier in black pyjamas, about to prod him with the ugly looking bayonet on her rifle.

"Look at this," he says to himself in one of the crammed magasins of remaindered books in Rue de Nesles, as a biography of Kurt Cobain falls open on a strange quote: "Birds are reincarnated old men with Tourette syndrome . . . "

Hey now . . . Oh hell, and this: "William and I sitting across from each other at a table, lots of blinding sun from the windows behind us . . . He gropes me from behind and falls dead on top of me. Medical footage of sperm flowing through penis. A ghost vapor comes out of his groin and enters my body." Treatment for "Heart-Shaped Box" video, 1992. He is talking of Wm. Burroughs.

At 6:18 PM he is standing at the northern side rail of the deserted pedestrian Pont des Arts facing the Vert Galant, two listless anglers crouched on canvas folding chairs and the inevitable kissing couple leaning against one of the trees — in the shimmering heat he cannot tell whether it's a guy and a girl, or two guys, or what — and he feels ready to fold forward and plop into the river and just let it happen.

Did I Say That? Do You Remember?

"I think maybe I could use a hip therapist who's into child-hood traumatization, that sort of thing," Alain says in El-vira's living-room on Place de Furstemberg; and she comes back with: "I know a neurologist at the American Hospital. Great guy to hang out with."

"If you can fix me up with him I'll take him."

"He was a consultant on that movie about the kid who watched his parents getting whacked —he was hiding in the dumb-waiter —and has stopped talking. And the cops are getting impatient, and Richard Dreyfus isn't getting anywhere with him."

Alain hasn't been listening. "Think I'll take the slow ap-proach . . . "

"Meaning . . . "

"The Bus." He appears to be lost in thought. "The 82, from Gare Montparnasse to the entrance of the Emergency Room on Avenue Victor Hugo . . . "

"You've been there . . . "

"I was going to kill somebody and forgot all about it because I had a great idea for a book —which I never wrote. Wasted trip. You want to kill somebody, never ride on a bus with them for an hour. You're bound to get distracted."

There is an original Jacques Monory hanging above her Moroccan sofa. The title is *Murder #11*.

"I can't seem to raise Ed on his cell phone," he adds as an afterthought.

"He's back on heroin."

"Oh."

"Somebody stole his car. That was the last straw."

Razzia sur la Chnouf

When they carried Albert Cossery out of Room 58 he was ninety-four and his eyelids looked as thin as silk paper, traced with tiny fading blue veins. On the stairs they moved right through the astral body of Detective-Lieutenant Connor. "He was indecently successful with mulattos of both sexes," says Anais the receptionist.

Here's Rimbaud skipping through the rain, and although he carries no umbrella he reaches No.10, Rue de Buci completely dry, as if he had been recently unfolded from a camphor chest. "And I marked the thin elastic spittle, like the linkage of a mussel to its shell, joining his upper to his lower lip."

Laurin is standing at the window on the left looking across the grey sunbleached corrugated tin roofs, the noise of the streets only a distant murmur, and there is the dull feeling that maybe he is running dry. He has been wandering around all day, oblivious to his surroundings, bumping into people and getting shoved aside by delivery men, and nothing has come to him.

He might as well light a candle at the feet of the Black Madonna in St. Sulpice and complain to her, in a pissed and grating tone of voice, "Where's my raison d'être, goddammit?"

And she, supremely bored, without missing a beat: "Thass sump'n we is fresh out of, Bro' . . . " It's the old story. As soon as you run out of things to say, everybody gets hostile.

Any Raghead Deadbeat Can Get His 15 Minutes

Around 3 AM on Friday morning two SWAT teams secured the front and the back of 96, rue Myrha. It was an old three-storey building on the slowly ascending quiet upper part of the street, on the fringe of the African quarter called Goutte d'Or.

The old-time brasserie on the ground floor had closed several months ago. To the left and right of it were uninviting dolorous stores selling clothes made in Senegal and Benin, hairdryers, cheap trinkets, fetish stones on leather thongs, and transistor radios made to look like Pepsi cans.

Two security experts came up the stairs leading to the basement and whispered into the team leader's ear that the door of the bomb factory as well as the narrow corridor leading to it were not rigged with alarm systems of any kind; and that they were fairly sure that the door was booby-trapped on the inside.

On the previous afternoon, while the two Algerians had been out, they had drilled a tiny hole in the lowest part of the door. With a fiber-optic device they had just now verified that one of the Algerians was asleep while the other was sitting at a table reading a magazine.

At a nod from the team leader, one of the technicians cautiously led the guy with the canister of nerve gas down the steps. Neither was wearing a gas mask. It was too hot, even at three in the morning, and the sweat running into their eyes would have ruined their concentration.

A tiny Maglite with a red filter showed the way. Their advance was painfully slow and sawed at everybody's nerves. When they were crouching in front of the door, the one with the gas switched off the Mag. He unrolled a thin plastic tube from the canister and pushed it through the hole in the door which had been hidden by a speck of putty.

The pressure inside the canister was low so that the gas would make no noise as it was delivered. It took them forever to feed enough nerve gas into the room to kill the two terrorists.

The operation was considered a spectacular success. There was so much that could have gone wrong.

Shortly after 8 AM, just as the President was bragging about it in a statesman-like way, No. 96 blew up.

They had evacuated half of the block and installed, in the basement of No. 94, a driller robot operated by remote control. It had broken through the wall of ancient brick and set off the garland of boobytraps strung around the room.

And when the refrigerator disintegrated, the bombs in the freezer compartment went off.

A Clean Well-Lighted Place

The Deux Magots spends about 500 bucks a day on lilies. A huge bouquet greets you as you walk in, and in the early morning, with no more than five or six customers in the place, the bewitching scent will waft past your nose "in the comparatively fresh air" (F. Kafka).

This morning Alain happened to sit in the corner where they have a framed picture of Hemingway and Janet Flanner on the wall. Both are in uniform, and the Flanner woman actually looks like Bloody Brygyda from Auschwitz-Monowitz.

On the Place St.-Germain-des-Prés, right in front of the church, a bearded zealot was selling an Islamist propaganda sheet modeled after Sartre's "La Cause du Peuple" of 1970. It was called "Nightmare of the Infidels."

Around the corner from the Deux Magots they were redoing the ground floor etablissement above the legendary former Club St. Germain —the signature square blue door was already gone —where Alain had once sat through two sets of Art Blakey and The Jazz Messengers, with Valerij Ponomarev on trumpet. Valerij who loved the English language for its limitless stock of snappy remarks. "Gimme an F, shit-for-brains" he says to the piano player.

Aiming along the length of his knife (Millefeuille with apricot mush, tiède, had to be handled with a knife and fork) Alain led passers-by for a second or two and muttered to himself: "Is he going to draw down on you? And you? And . . . you?" He felt a need to hurry up and get the story written or he might lose interest in his main character.

In the color supplement of the liberal German weekly somebody was quoting an overeducated bouncer with the immortal words: "Feminism was invented to help integrate ugly women into society." And tonight, he read in Le Parisien, at the Salle André Malraux in Sarcelles, they were expecting an all-girl grunge band called "J'vas enterrer ta bite" (I'll bury your dick).

The Five Minute Rule

When Laurin got off the #1 at Hôtel de Ville and looked back over his shoulder he recognized two men and a woman who had followed him down the steps at Louvre Rivoli in that deliberate way they all have toward the end of a surveillance when they finally want you to make them —unobtrusively spaced, yet somehow close together so they'll be able to get on the same train with you. He followed the crowd into the tiled corridor that led directly into the basement of the Bazar de l'Hôtel de Ville. It was no use trying to lose them in the department store. His only thought was: "Lose them in five." It was like a blinking pop-up sign in the back of his head. He had tried to heed the five minute rule ever since reading about it in a book on trade craft.

He made for an exit marked "Employees Only" and ran up
the stairs to the street where salesgirls liked to loiter on the
sidewalk and puff away. It was close to 7 PM and the Rue des
Archives was full of gays heading for their daily powwow in
front of the Coxring, a new water-and-grope hole painted
fire-truck red.

Diagonally across from the Cox, he stood at the entrance of
the Pain Quotidien for a beat, then veered left and squeezed
through the gap between the potted bamboo and the wall
and disappeared into the Lutheran church, a semi-detached
affair not immediately recognizable as a church. In a sort
of cloister they were hosting an exhibition of bad sculpture.
Behind a large ugly piece made of taffeta and long strips of
plastic he unhooked an ancient door and followed a narrow
unlit corridor to an exit on the other side.

He crossed the back street and went straight into the show-
room of Azzedine Alaia, a former market with an ornate
glass roof supported by slim cast-iron columns. At the far
end he slipped through a service door and reached a small
court.

There was a delivery truck parked near the street entrance,
and next to it there were several shoulder-high rectangular
garbage containers. He knocked on them until he found
one that wasn't full. He climbed in, closed the lid, settled
in a comfortable position on the soft vinyl bags and tried
not to feel claustrophobic.

Avenging Ghosts
of the Llano Estacado

Most of the 400 people on the square in front of Notre Dame on this Saturday afternoon were tourists strolling around or sitting on the massive stone benches on three sides of the Place du Parvis N.D., eating snacks or aiming their cameras at the cathedral which after extensive sandblasting looked incongruously . . . new.

The twelve Black Widows in flowing chadors, their faces not veiled, came from three different directions in groups of three and two. Half of them were carrying, in addition to the triple-cascade C4 harness around the midriff, elaborate nail bombs that looked like auxiliary parachutes on their backs.

They converged on the center of the square and formed a circle, holding hands. Almost instantly, they were detonated by radio signal.

The signal came from an old model Motorola C200 cell phone.

The blast ruptured eardrums as far away as the pedestrian crossing on Rue de la Cité and swept about a dozen children and adults down the wide steps leading to the Crypte Archéologique.

Most of the people on the square appeared to get yanked sideways or outward as if on invisible ropes. About 130 of them were dead before they hit the ground.

In the horizontal hail of screws and nails from the bombs, at least fifteen children who had been feeding the birds fluttering above the low privet hedges bordering the square on the side facing the Left Bank were torn to pieces.

A photographer, his face flecked with blood, his hands shaking, took a picture of a kid's rucksack studded with nails and with the kid's headless torso still attached to it.

The silence following the blast lasted approximately three seconds; enough for survivors to become aware of a helicopter with a large white cross on its bottom hovering overhead. Somebody, secured by a harness, was leaning out shooting video of the carnage.

After that, panic. A chilling chorus of piercing cries. Chaos.

Half of the large glass front of the Hôtel Dieu entrance (oldest Paris hospital), on the left as you look toward Notre Dame, was shattered. Within sixty seconds of the detonation, doctors, nurses and orderlies with stretchers were rushing out.

A young intern sank to her knees next to a man bleeding from a bad neck wound caused by a flying shard of plate glass. He was alternately gasping and gurgling. Without a second's hesitation she plucked out the shard and intubated her patient through the open wound.

Hysterical survivors, one of them a cop, were seen stomping upon the severed heads of three of the Widows. Many survivors looked strangely disfigured and leprous. It was the blood and shredded entrails of the victims clinging to their arms and faces.

The wave of the blast entered Notre Dame through the three tall doors which were wide open. Inside, it blew out candles left and right.

There was no visible damage to the famous stained-glass rosetta on the front of the cathedral.

Less than half an hour after the blast, the footage shot from the fake medevac chopper appeared on an Islamist website ("Regard, oh brothers, the glorious battleground . . . !") It was copied and uploaded on YouTube and elsewhere dozens of times right away.

On Sunday —inexplicably, since the Place du Parvis Notre Dame and its surroundings were cordoned off —a huge banner was unrolled from the balustrade above the rosetta of the cathedral: PAS DE VIERGES AU PARADIS!

It was considered a particularly heinous outrage in the Muslim world as it seemed to suggest that the twelve martyrs had been lesbians.

There was a mass exodus of tourists from Paris. There was vicious vigilante action against brownskinned persons in various parts of the city. The President, foaming and sputtering, addressed the nation from a secret location underneath a mountain somewhere.

Radio Beur, a Maghreb FM station with studios in the 18th Arrondissement, had gone ballistic with pride and joy. It had received a visit from the Police du Raid which left the equipment in pieces, the owners and staff in the basement of the Préfecture de Police for marathon sessions of torture and interrogation.

Within a day or two, jihadists were broadcasting hate sermons from mobile pirate stations all over town.

Alain Laurin, feeling clipped behind the knees by the Fates, decided to move the Sniper story to Cairo.

The Cairo Caper.
Dermott McCarthy Reporting.

"In Cairo the air was hot and still and brown and heavy. The Sniper had gotten himself a deep tan on the Tunisian peninsula of Djerba where he had stayed at the Hotel El Bousten. He was wearing native garb and blending in rather well in the Egyptian capital, except for his feet which were not sufficiently scuffed and calloused. On the other hand, staring at a person's feet was considered impolite in those countries ... "

Lansky looked up and laughed and handed the notebook back. "You're right. This could go on and on ... Le Snaypeur doesn't like the idea of having to compete with a bunch of other-directed Fatimas, so he decides to hit the Muslim brothers where they live. In situ! Bismillah!"

Pardon Me, Guvnor, Is This the Bognor Regis Choo-Choo

"The brain is a wonderful instrument. Until God decides to chew on it." Hunter S. Thompson.——In his dusty office in the rear sous-sol of the American Hospital, with access to the garden and its sprinklered lawns and huge chestnut trees, Dr. Michel Denard leans back and says, politely but firmly: "In plain English, M'sieu Laurin, you can't have your publisher's car stolen by one of your characters. Unless you know something that no one else . . . "

"Meaning," Alain cuts in, "we should go on the assumption that my brain isn't working right."

"Let's. Yes."

"We're getting off on the wrong foot here."

"I agree." The doctor pours another generous splash of rather good bourbon over the ice cubes in Alain's glass. "Lansky's sports car was stolen in real life —just as, in the book you're writing, the same car got stolen by your main character . . . "

"Exact same spot, too."

"Right. A strange coincidence. If you believe in coincidences."

"I don't believe in anything."

"Good. We have to keep an open mind about these things."

Leaving the hospital, his brain awash with dire possibilities, he absently wandered the luxuriously shadowed streets of Neuilly, down to the river . . . and felt the temperature go up a notch or two, followed by an onset of vertigo and a tightening sensation around the chest . . . He recognized the fragrant air clinging to his sweating skin, the smells of fish, hawkers' fires and jasmin, the salty mud flats at the creeks . . . and all that coral-blue sea out there. Fifty years ago, Penang must have been like paradise, he thought —some bungalows here and there, dusty casuarinas, but mostly the giddy smell of a still-unpolluted sea . . . Ah, and there was the Eastern & Oriental, used to be a very pukka-sa-hib sort of place, famous like Raffles in Singapore, favored by Residents, rajahs and Twickenham Duchesses, cheh! who would gather on the lawn on Friday night to complain about their servants . . .

A nest of flotsam drifted by, populated by starving fire ants, having circled about in the final days of the monsoon . . . "This," said the Tamil as he unlocked the padlock and un-wound the heavy chain, "is a disaster area."

The road had dwindled to twin tyre tracks which curved around until all view of the sea was lost. Here, at the back of the hill, there was no breeze. The jungle was very still . . . ferns, vines everywhere, tall trees with buttressed roots pressing so insistently against the ten-foot barbed wire fence that the concrete posts were tilting inwards . . . Laurin, lost in space, searched his pockets like an epileptic, located the Motorola and called his neurologist. "Guess what."

"Laurin?"

"Guess what."

"What?"

"I'm in Malaysia."

"Very funny."

"No, it's not. I'm in the jungle. Just north of Penang, to be precise."

"You left my office less that half an hour ago, and now you are in Penang? You must be nuts."

"That may be so, but I'm not here because I want to be. That makes me a dangerous nut."

"I see."

"You do, huh? So get me out of here, toubib."

"Maybe it's your Karma to . . . "

"No. It's a fuckin' concentration camp. Dead bodies all over, rotting away. Get me out of here."

"I'll see what I can do."

"Not good enough."

"It'll have to do."

"Tell you what. Give me twenty minutes, I'm back, running Amok in your fine fuckin' hospital, clutching a kris. Which IN MALAYSIA, in case you didn't know, is the weapon of choice when you're contemplating . . . a run."

A. falls out of bed and bolts awake.Trying to fend off some crazed characters whose brown teeth were glistening with blood he has bruised his right hand on the rickety nightstand. He hates dreams in which his body refuses to obey him. But what can you do.

Mullah Got Himself on a Shitlist

The backyard mosque was in the Rue Saint Luc, a short narrow street leading to the Eglise St. Mathieu, in the Eighteenth. The house in back was a sagging decrepit building with a clothing and knick-knack store on the ground floor that was doing no visible business.

On the nearest corner there was a tea and couscous place called Soleil Maghrebin. From the street market around the other corner crawled the sickly-sweet smell of fish and mutton about to turn.

The mosque enjoyed a certain underground reputation for selling propaganda DVDs showing western hostages getting their head cut off, and 12-year-old Jewish girls getting fucked up the ass and stabbed to death in a frenzy of flying blood.

Several teenage members of the Belleville Social and Athletic Club, who saved old folks from death by desiccation during the day and firebombed the homes of hate preachers at night, met behind Saint Mathew's at 11:55 PM. They wore black T-shirts with HEALTH ANGELS stenciled on the back in a phosphorescent likeness of Nordic runes . . .

Exhumación
del Cadáver de Pablo Escobar

"I'm out getting drunk with whores tonight but give me a call tomorrow." (Voice mail from Joselito)——Half of the French bestseller list that week consisted of comic books. Half of the Japanese bestseller list consisted of novels written on cell phones.

Norma Rivington's book wasn't doing nearly well enough. Lansky, with a shrug: "Actually, what caught my interest was that the creeps lived somewhere on the river —Shepperton? Sunbury? One of those Ratty, Toad and Mole places out to the West. Did you know that a German writer, rather esteemed back home but a terrible bore, lived on an island in the Thames? A feeble attempt to emulate Pat Highsmith who lived on an island in the Loire. Anyway, they found him dead, with half of his body already rotted away. Fucking Krauts will stink up the place wherever they can . . . "

"Asking for it, aren't we?" says the Secretary of the Interior and orders all cops on vacation or sick-leave back to the job and out into the streets. "My hatred of the racaille is second to none." What a windbag.

The waitress at the Bouillon des Colonies on Rue Racine is in her late thirties, and Alain notes that with her black horn-rimmed glasses she looks like Marguerite Duras at the time when Madame helped torture that traitor and in the process realized she wanted to get screwed by him.

The silence in St. Sulpice was oppressive. Something to do

with the temperature drop as you come in from the heat, he decided. The light in the stained-glass windows was dimming, shadows growing everywhere, and the sort of cold only churches can harbor was coming up from the flagstone floor.

Earlier that day, the Sniper had witnessed a big rig jack-knife on the Périphérique, spilling its load of Bermuda shorts and running shoes. A beur family had stopped their car and were trying on shoes, oblivious to the cars zipping past them . . . Now he reached for the light switch and flipped it on. In the corner, a large bird cage lay tipped over on its side. The grey parrot inside began shrieking and flapping its wings . . .

He walked to the front of the bed. Whatever struggle had knocked the cage to the floor had started here. The mattress had been pulled to the side, blanket and top sheet were on the floor, the fitted sheet on the mattress had been pulled nearly off and torn down the center . . .

They had tied her with duct tape and carried her out, knocking the picture in the hallway and cracking the glass. What violence does to a place, the story it leaves in everyday objects, is sometimes more frightening than the evidence left on a body.

There are now six low olive-drab buildings on Place d'Estienne d'Orves, identical metal prefabs clustered according to exact specifications, separated by roadways of uniform width with white-painted curbs. They are ringed by a tall razor-wire fence that continues west to enclose a parking lot. There are three armoured personnel carriers and several black Humvees in the lot, each with a quick-release machinegun mount on top.

The gate is a white counterbalanced pole with a guard shack next to it, a corrugated metal affair with windows on all four sides. Four guys are in it, dressed in desert BDUs and boots, armoured vests and helmets.

The square in front of Notre Dame, after a serious effort to clean it up and get rid of the blood stains, is a sea of rotting flowers, with the occasional teddy bear leaking sawdust, and, from a lone ghetto-blaster, Celine Dion belting out "Near! Far! Wherever you are!"

A lot of bleach has been used on the flagstones of the square, yet nobody will tread on them. The wearing of chadors, niqabs, djellabahs and burkhas has been outlawed.

Dear Diary: Take This.

Nazis dans le Métro. A novel by Gerard Guégan in the window of La Hune. Laurin is hit by a whiff of envy.

"After the event in front of the church," says Brigitte, " —what's next? Blowing the Virgin Megastore out of the water?"

"Don't think so," says Alain.

"Hnf. You listen to my Dad, the grown-up thing to do is look after your Paris real estate while the air is filling up with Cesium and Strontium-90.

'I want OUT of this fucken town', I say.

An' he's like 'Well, I can probably get you into a boarding school run by Coptic nuns in Switzerland. Swanky place, from what I hear . . . '

'Here's where I lose it', I say. You should have heard him laugh."

She fiddles with her dreadlocks. "You and I," she says with an exaggerated look from under, "we're the only ones who are not in denial."

Let's Hear It for Rabbit Hash, Kentucky

Elvira, looking up from her newspaper: "Am I plagued by the leprosy of the affluent?"

Ed Lansky: "Define leprosy."

Elvira (tenderly): "Fuck you."

The cook serves the hare. Which has been simmering in a kilo of mirabelles for three hours. Within seconds everybody is singing the cook's praise. Her face contorts into a grimace of self-consciousness. "You're supposed to throw a faint from the smell alone," she says grumpily.

"I'm such a pig when it comes to food, mate," says Ed, his mouth full.

Elvira grabs the bottle of St. Raphael and takes a gulp. "This stuff dies painless with me. It never knows what hit it." She is a repository of Chandlerisms.

"You notice we're avoiding The Subject," says Elvira's niece, Bernadette (a/k/a Betty) who has a degree in enology and is running the family's vineyards in Burgundy. Her Crémant de Bourgogne is considered exceptional. It is also ruthlessly expensive.

"Suits me," says Alain. He mentions that the Minister of Foreign Affairs, a faggot with a double name, has stated that Italy reminds him of a fat man on a vibrating bed.

Elvira is not impressed. "That hyphenated fruit."

"Two desks to the left of my Mom in the lycée in Grenoble," says Betty. "He was a softy even then. A finger poked in anywhere on him would have sunk to the second knuckle."

Her tongue is as sharp as her aunt's. She drives a red Mini Cooper with heated rearview mirrors because her skiing lodge in the Savoy Alps is at an altitude somewhat above ten-thousand feet. For depilation she has platinum membership (appointments at 3 AM, etc.) chez "Wax in the City"; and she has recently shot a commercial for "Hydra Zen Neurocalm Gel Essence," an anti-stress ultra-moisturizing product by Lancôme.

Her partners in the Crémant business are five Japanese investors who will occasionally let on that they have no use for "your decadent savoi-weef-leh." She calls them The Kon-Ichiwà Bitches.

"I gotta say this," says the cook as she serves the flan, the madeleines, and the coffee. "Watching Brigitte Bardot, gone to fat, in a shapeless muumuu . . . on crutches! a geriatric wreck!" Her speech is a little slurred, and she walks unsteadily. "In front of that judge who for the umpteenth time, okay? slaps a fine of fifteen-thousand Euro on her for making racist remarks . . . "

"Aw, spare me that grassy-knoll feminism," drawls Lansky, cracking everybody up. "All she needs to do is get a sex change, and they'll pin a medal on her. Let's write her a letter: 'Be a Man!' . . . "

Reconstitution de la Mort de Dalida

When Laurin left the hotel around eight in the morning he noticed that more homeless people than usual were sleeping on the sidewalks, in doorways of condemned buildings, in the entrance of a bank that wouldn't open before 10 o'clock.

"They don't speak a word of French, or English," said a shop-keeper. "No papers, no nationality. I guess that makes it difficult to deport them. Of course, we could herd them into detention camps, along with them A-rabs." He put his left thumb to his left nostril and loosened a gob in the direction of a Bulgarian ex-fisherman (a chemical plant having poisoned the lower Danube) snoring between two garbage cans. "Never happen. Not in my lifetime."

"I remember reading that there are eighty-thousand people living on top of a garbage dump in Manila," says Alain.

The man's face darkens. "You sayin' this à propos of nothing or what?"

"And they say that there's a million people who sleep every night in the cemeteries of Cairo."

The man has heard enough. "What are you, a census taker on the skids? Get away from me . . . you, you . . . !"

Of course the real news is that there are a billion people worldwide who live in cardboard boxes and other makeshift housing, in "unplanned communities," off the grid, off the economy, off the map. According to the New York Times Style Magazine.

The immediate bringdown of the day, however, was —in the window of an art gallery on Rue Dauphine —an overpriced kitsch painting of a gondola carrying two passengers covered with snow, and a gondoliere with melting snowflakes sliding down his face . . . St. Silvester's night in Venice, the gray-green water, the Aduana and the entrance to the Canale Grande; the restaurants crowded with Slavic mafiosi and their blond women; Chinese tourists shivering with cold as a colorful display of fireworks explodes over La Giudecca . . . Then, once again, the glow of lights through the fog and pale flakes falling on the canals, tongues of water lapping over white stone steps and washing in gentle waves across marble paving . . . A sense of dread and foreboding . . . La Serenissima has reached the Zero Degree of Desolation . . .

One of the widow trainers made a call from a public phone in the lobby of a movie theater on Rue Galande to a bistro in the Seventeenth where the receiver was handed to the secret service agent who was running him. The message was brief.

"Make another call before you leave," said the agent. "Don't leave this as the last number called."

They hung up.

A Prolonged Misfiring of the Synapses

Tous ces mots partis en fumée . . . (Cocteau/OPIUM)——KILL A DIAPER-HEAD FOR JESUS! The slogan had been printed on plain white laser printer paper by someone probably using a fine-point sharpie. "Block printing," said the detective, "is not easy. Right-handed, I'd guess . . . "

There was a reminder in the communist daily L'Humanité of the fact that Algerian special forces had impersonated Islamist rebels, staging rapes and massacres of women and children to mobilize public support for military rule.

Reading this had a chilling effect on A. and let him forget the noon heat for a while. He was looking at a huge yellowed poster for a concert at the Olympia:

*** LIVE ON STAGE *** FROM PALMA'S PURO BEACH *** ISIS "APACHE" MONTERO *** . . . and drew a blank. For a second or two he had thought he'd made a connection to something Dr. Denard had mentioned.

It was only natural. The Doc had offered him a choice of two technical terms, one German, one Spanish: "Aussetzer" and "ataques olvidadores."

Don't Burn the House Nigger Goddammit

Someone has soaked a sleeping bag with a vagrant in it with gasoline and dropped a match on it. The vag happened to camp out in front of the floor-to-ceiling safety glass window offering a view of the Louisiane's front desk.

The flames have melted the lower part of the window, and the smoke has blackened the facade above it.

The guy on night duty ran away when he realized that he didn't know how to operate the fire extinguisher.

The fire stopped by itself when the vag had burned to the shape and color of a chicken left to smolder in the oven.

Free Man in Paris

In the waiting room downstairs at the American Hospital they look emaciated from too many long hours on uncomfortable aluminum chairs, eating machine snacks and drinking powdered coffee and synthetic whitener.

There is a boy of sixteen or so, looks like he got hit by lightning —hair turned into a fright wig, smoke curling out from between his toes —his legs jerking up and down even though he's got his arms around his knees. Restless Legs Syndrome. An awful condition; etiology unknown.

Alain has read up on it in the hospital library, over in the Florence Gould wing.

"What're you getting for your RLS?" he asks. One must pretend an interest.

"Di-hydro-oxy-codeine," says the boy without looking at him.

"Which doesn't do it for you anymore. Doesn't mean you've run out of options, though."

"Oh no," the boy says, tonelessly. Everything about him spells bleak. "There's heroin . . . start off at seventeen percent pure, go up all the way . . . "

"Then there's di-hydro-oxy-heroin. Supposed to be a hundred times stronger than . . . "

"Right. It's really endless." A horrible smile is crawling across the boy's face. Disgust you to see it.

Cat Piss in the Privet Hedge

Aw shit, he mutters to himself in the little park near the Sèvres-Babylone subway station where he is filling another notebook with plot absurdities and the stumbling progress of his main character on 2 (two) missions at once: Now that his ex-wife has been abducted, the Sniper is mutating into a killer virus with shoes, 100% unpredictable. Not that he has any deep feelings for her, but he does feel plenty of hatred for those who kidnapped her.

The salty sweat drops falling from the tip of his nose splatter on the pages of Alain's notebook, and the incessant traffic noise penetrates the thick designer vegetation of the park with the ease of a knife through warm butter. And the smell of cat piss in the privet hedge is his maddening madeleine for today. He is certain that he has never been to Malaysia and yet the smells and odors are rushing at him, challenging him to remember . . .

Not just the Chinese wet markets, but also the alien mixture of charcoal smoke and spice and sewer and two-stroke exhaust and the sweet mouldy aroma of those broad-leafed tropical weeds and grasses . . .

He'd have preferred walking the streets in the cool morning as the Sikh bank guards were eating barfi and drinking cow's milk on the sidewalk —yes, there were sidewalks in downtown Kuala Kangsar . . . "Really just arrived. Outstation, as they say. Look, here comes the satay. Probably loaded with parasites . . . "

In the yellow nimbus of the carbide lamps above the stalls and trolleys of the vendors you could see and smell the damp as it mixed with the odors of sandalwood and curry and excrement. In the distance there were a few sodium streetlamps and in the liquid dark beneath the mangoes one could see the glistening possum eyes of Malay men and boys . . .

He made an involuntary gesture as if he were swatting at a bunch of bluebottles.

Ach Franz, Muss das Jetzt Sein

The guards at the Vel d'Hiv shuffled their feet restlessly. A., who considered his situation hopeless, stood at attention and waited. Ten-thousand Aliens sat on the bleachers of the former arena for six-day bicycle races, focussing their hatred on him.

"Alain Schultz," said a voice from behind the screen. The voice, thin, flat and emotionless, came through a small amplifier. A. could barely understand the words. Tone and inflection were lost: Even in speaking the judge remained anonymous.

" . . . but speaking from the viewpoint of the state, I will tell you that an addicted populace is a loyal populace; that drugs are a major source of tax revenue; that drugs exemplify our entire way of life . . . "

"You're keeping the Man from Nirvana standing on a windy

roof," A. raised his voice. "Is there anyone smart enough to lead us to this conference room?"

"I'm Full of Knife Scars."
Angelina Jolie

Brigitte, in spite of the relentless heat, is wearing long-sleeved men's shirts. She has been cutting herself for five months now.

"What the hell," she says in the Häagen Dasz on Rue de Bussy. "Did you see that video clip—they have since removed it—of Angelina Jolie at the Actors Studio where she tells the story of how during sex with her first boyfriend at age 13, ahm, somehow it didn't feel like enough, so she starts cutting him with a kitchen knife? And he cuts her right back . . . Voilà."

In English 101 she has been assigned Susan Sontag's "Project for a Trip to China."

"Listen to this: 'Inside the hole, I scraped out a niche in the east wall, where I set a candle. I sat on the floor. Dirt fell through the cracks between the planks into my mouth . . .' She's bragging about her disturbed ways at eleven years old . . . out in the Southwest . . . where nobody's ever heard the word psychiatrist . . . "

Alain hasn't touched his Macadamia Nut Brittle.

"Landlord comes by in his jeep, tells her mom the hole has to be filled in. She fills it in. The maid helps her. Three months later she digs it again: 'I got three of the five Fuller kids across the road to help me. I promised them they could sit in the hole whenever I wasn't using it.' Who would want—as a reward!—to sit in a fucken hole in the ground?"

"Beats me," says Alain.

Bleeding Steadily into the Mud

Eventually, the frivolous mood collapses. The dinner table is a Daniel Spoerri battlefield. The cook, ivre-morte, has passed out in the bathroom. It is 9.30 PM. Joselito arrives, hungover and looking sickly pale in his slate-grey three-piece René Lezard suit. Trying to gauge the level of moroseness in the room, he does the unwelcome —wax philosophical and broach The Subject . . .

Joe: "How do a group of nouveaux riches deal with the threat of having their city fucked up by a dirty bomb? Answer: They don't. They sit around the dinner table with a queasy feeling, but they avoid . . . "

Elvira: "And there's a reason for that —why terrorize yourself when there are folks who will do it for you?"

Joe, after a beat: "There's that."

Ed Lansky has been on the nod and now comes out of it and for some reason confronts Alain as though continuing an argument of half an hour ago: "And I maintain that it is not quite natural for a guy around fifty who's never had sex with a live woman before to look at a 14-year-old" — Brigitte Mayat has turned fourteen that week — "and get funny ideas."

"As bad an approach to sex as any." Elvira picks up a partridge bone and throws it at Alain. "You hear what I'm saying?" —— "I'm supposed to drive you to the Crazy Horse for the late show," Joe reminds her.

"Quedase con su caballo loco!" Her voice is getting shrill.

Joe turns to Lansky. "What you mean, 'live women' — he's been shtupping dead ones?"

"Y-y-yeas, something like that."

"I'm into sex with robots," Alain explains. "Intermittently."

"Oh."

"Yes. Of course, Susan Sontag didn't know bupkes."

"If you say so."

A Little Entropy
Ain't Gonna Hurt Shit

Alain's notebook, more often than not, remains static for days. Then, all of a sudden, there is a new entry, usually nothing to do with the book he is trying to write:

"The M.E. death investigator took his pictures and then laid the dismembered guy back together. I said: "What you doing that for?" ... "Make sure the parts match." ... Hey shit, huh?" Elmore Leonard, *Mr. Paradise* (2004)

Everything around him seems to shrink and congeal. It's not writer's block exactly. It's an icky reluctance to continue in a profession that doesn't feel right.

"Maybe arson is my true calling after all," he says to himself. Followed by a mirthless chuckle.

Totally Green Troops in the Area

The Mayor has proclaimed Alien Nation Day, and the slimy creatures are having a ball, soliciting in the streets, goosing the women, sliding their forked tongues into the ears of passers-by ...

Bruno Alioto is getting pissed. "He WHAT? I can't sell this! Tone it down, willya!?"

The Mob Stirred Menacingly And Vomited. (Claude Pélieu)

On some days, to escape the sweltering stifling air, he goes into St. Sulpice and lies down on the floor. Others are already lying there. The sacristan is handing out plastic bottles of Evian. The organist is practising a passacaglia by Clérambault. An altogether restful situation. Except when two people are making out in one of the confessionals.

Maybe, he thinks, sheer professionalism demands that I move to Cairo and write the rest of the story there . . .

"The slum across the Nile from the fashionable district of Zamalek is so crowded its skewed tenement buildings often collapse beneath the weight of their occupants. The unpaved alleys have no names and are in perpetual darkness.

They run with raw sewage and are choked with mounds of garbage. At night they are ruled by packs of wild dogs.

The children wear rags, drink from puddles of brackish water and sleep light because of the rats.

There is no running water, very little electricity, and less hope. Only Islam. It is written on the crumbling walls in green spray paint: ISLAM IS THE ANSWER . . . "

Right. Yawn. He remembers the day he saw the ultimate Cairo yarn on Lansky's desk. By a former Far-East Correspondent of ITV, London. "Rommel's Nazis are goose-stepping into Cairo! Achtung! That's for me!" The book had been a flop.

This Movie Has No Emergency Exit

I won't feel relieved when I finish this book, he thinks. It's not that kind of story.

And the history of his ah predicament which Mike Denard is so eager to ferret out and eventually publish — is it worth the time and effort?

"Childhood traumatization," someone said in one of the papers he's been reading, "is a movie that has no emergency exit." There is no cure, only precarious survival. For a while.

He has slumped a little in his armchair at the Fumoir, on Place du Louvre. The waitress hesitates before she shakes him by the upper arm. "You all right?"

He jerks his arm away. "No, but . . . gimme another cranberry juice with prosecco."

"Now you're talking."

He looks at her ass sashaying away from him and mumbles to himself: "I'll kill you before I kill myself."

You keep this up, Alain Laurin, you'll be doing a lot of slumping in threadbare leather armchairs the world over.

The cracked dark brown leather is sweaty to the touch. Building fronts, he has been noticing lately, seem to have acquired a coat of gluey transpiration. It is hard to see because it has no sheen. However, one misstep to the right and

you'll wind up stuck to the wall like a fucking death's-head moth to a strip of flypaper.

Hit Men
Sleeping in Shabby Hotels
Covered with Bloody Dust.
(Pélieu)

The Sniper barges into a poker game in the back room of La Mère Lachaise, a pub near the main entrance of the Père Lachaise cemetery. He is out of breath and his face is glistening with perspiration.

"Keep your hands on the table. You know who I am. You know my ex-wife because she used to be your fence. I want to know who got her."

It is an unreal scene, all ambergris, blind mirror, verdigris. Gelatinous rain seems to be oozing down the window.

There is Mathieu-la-Valise, there's Joe-le-Taxi, there's Mimi Pattes-en-l'air, and Gouloub le Terroriste Introverti. They endeavor to look non-committal.

Die Like an Egyptian

Most of the killing had been done on the bed. It was drenched in blood and there were jet sprays all over the wall above the headboard.

They had hit the Egyptian with axes, and from the gore on the wall you could tell that two or three of them had gone to it. You could see blood-soaked adhesive tape where they had splayed him to the bedposts to work on his soft areas.

The ghosts of Connor and his Japanese partner followed the blood trail leading to the bathroom. They noted a broad but old bare back and sinewy muscles. The Egyptian still wore his suit pants. White linen, soaked through. The head was skewed to the right. A bandage of electrician's tape locked a wad of cotton into his silent mouth. The visible eye was open wide in horror, and the face seemed to be floating in blood.

Connor stared. Why the hell would he crawl in here? Why die on a bathroom floor? Why roll off the bed and crawl, dragging your guts and lungs and spleen into the . . .

He followed the man's splayed left arm and saw the hand end in a finger pointing —no, writing. Three crude letters, the satiny black blood seeping out of the ravaged body about to engulf them: DST.

"In situations like this," said the Jap, "I hate to be dead."

Connor looked at him (or through him, depending on your point of view): "You're so pathetic, you know that?"

Cigarette Smoking Woman in Lingerie Stabbed to Death (YouTube)

Life in the city, in listless slow motion, is exhibiting aspects of 50s pulp SF. Dialog from *Alphaville* and *The Wind From Nowhere* probably would fit in seamlessly.

On the elevated métro tracks, with the train approachiing Bir Hakeim, Alain looked up from his tattered paperback . . . "I guess maybe Ballard wasn't so wrong after all . . . "

At the end of the month Colonel Riggs and his small holding unit would complete their survey of the city and set off northward, tow- ing the testing station with them . . . A giant Anopheles mosquito the size of a dragonfly spat through the muggy air past his face, then dived down towards the floating jetty where K's katamaran was moored, ten feet above the former main entrance of the Ritz . . .

Free Man in Paris (II)

The clandestini are roasting half a dog in the Jardin du Luxembourg. They are sitting around the fire, in the sand pit of a children's playground, their emaciated faces oily with rancid sweat.

It is a medieval scene, like the ones described by Jean Giono in *The Horseman on the Roof.* They could be survivors of the

Plague, ready to kill anybody trying to make a lunge for their stinking piece of meat.

The heatwave lasts and lasts, testing everybody's will to remain civilized. "Ça dure, ça dure" is the pitiful cry on the frontpage of Le Parisien.

"(I was a) Free Man in Paris" —Joni Mitchell. Oh hell yes. At The Pure Malt, opposite the Hôtel Caron where he was staying at the time, Alain had one day decided that the only free organism in Paris was the hookworm. There were too many people, himself included, who acted remote-controlled. It was, as the French say, pénible.

Anime Villainess in Miniskirt Whacked by Hitwoman

Late at night, A. happens to click on a video clip of JG Ballard doing an interview with BBC. The Man from Shepperton is surrounded by late 50s Cadillacs, all of them totaled.

"The future," he states, "is something with a fin on it."

It would be frightfully banal to assume that he is predicting a comeback of the tail fin. Instead . . . well, if you listen to the background music —it's Captain Beefheart: "Think I'll grow fins, go back in the water again . . . "

Not that it matters. Just an observation en passant.

He could jump out of that window on the left now. He doesn't.

He does remember a tea-colored paper napkin from The Pure Malt, which he had promptly lost, with some felt-pen 'Notes towards an Obituary':

"When the weather turned bad, he wrote an abrupt closing chapter for his novel.

Then he watched French B movies for two days.

Then, in an icy rain, he sat down on the curb near the Cluny La Sorbonne subway station and died."

Il Passato è una Terra Straniera

"Cremaster's amputee star Aimee Mullins lay half buried on the roof of a badly wrecked lime-green 1967 Chrysler Imperial, a gigantic white septic ball sticking out of the back like the abdomen of a spider . . . "

May 18, 2008, 6:30 P.M. PST at a defunct RV dealership south of Los Angeles.

One of the Erinnyas is back. He cannot tell which one. And for the first time he feels cornered. Threatened. Denied the oxygen in the air.

There is a sinking feeling, like pilot's vertigo, as he realizes that she must be the messenger that will mouth the dreaded words: Face the music and die.

"Her profile is Egyptian," he writes in his notebook. "The eyes glint like amber. The ocular fluid has the density of mercury. I am overcome by a sickening vertigo on seeing my reflection in the eyes of an alien.

I touch her cheek, experimentally, and it is like touching the taut cold skin of a serpent waiting for the sun to warm the desert sand.

I imagine she possesses some weird sort of sexuality and is insatiable. One can chart the progress of her arousal, from the accelerating spasms to the culminating climax. The explosion of long-drawn-out squeals occurs every one and a half minutes. It is sustained for twenty to thirty seconds. And the whole process begins again . . . "

Her name was Andromeda Parker. He didn't recall killing her. ———— A Japanese restaurant in the Ninth was offering Kobe steak grilled over Marie Antoinette's dead gingko tree.

Sins of the Cities of the Plain

"Dames en Heren, goden avond," said the 5′4 tourist guide. She was from Surinam, hence the fluency in Dutch, and majoring in medical law and forensic psychology at the Sorbonne.

Her clients on this August evening were disaster tourists from Amsterdam and Delft who had signed up for a Poetry-and-Terrorism tour of the Left Bank.

They were standing on the sidewalk opposite an apartment building on Rue Toullier.

"The two windows on the top floor," said the guide, "are where Rilke had the idea for his novel *Malte Laurids Brigge* in July 1903. We know this from a letter he wrote at the time to one of his aristocrat groupies in Italy.

"In 1975 the apartment on the second floor was rented by Nancy Sanchez, a Sorbonne student from Caracas. One of her Venezuelan acquaintances was a businessman who called himself Carlos Martinez.

"On June 27 there was a party in the apartment attended by Martinez, Nancy S. and some of her friends from the Cuban Embassy, and three guys from the DST, one of them the Middle East section chief.

"They made small talk for a while, then Martinez excused himself, went to the john, came back with a pistol and killed the three secret service agents.

"In the morning, he took the first plane to London, using the Venezuelan passport with his real name, Carlos Ramirez Sanchez. Shortly after that he became known as Carlos the Jackal.

"Let me mention in passing that the Rilke novel opens with a date and place:

"'11. September, rue Toullier . . .' Which translates into English as Nine-Eleven."

"I Bought a Pair of Ray-Bans from the Devil / And a Lighter Said Tu Do Bar 69 ... "

The killing spree of August 31 reminded some commentators of Darfur. "The first victim they found was a girl of thirteen. Her face was bashed in and her insides torn apart . . . "

The media, with customary hyperbole, called it the worst crime ever committed on French soil.

Alain Laurin didn't think that he had done it. But then.

Maybe if they had grabbed him off the street, given him the third degree stigmata. "No tiene memoria, eh? Hay que crearle una memoria . . . " So forth.

However, A. was not walking the streets: When he came to, on September 1, he was lying between shovels and cement sacks in a cubicle inside one of the concrete pillars of the Boulevard Périphérique somewhere out west. As far as he could tell, he had not been turned into a giant cockroach.

The place was occupied by an old guy who was completely hairless and seemed to be the taciturn sort. It took Alain a while before he realized that the man was deaf and dumb.

His face was gray, his breath rife with funk. He refused to use sign language. When Alain was in the way, he got shoved aside. When he made a hungry face, he was thrown a bologna sandwich. It soon became apparent that the man considered him his prisoner.

"Did you know that pigeon shit contains saltpeter?" he writes on a piece of paper and thrusts it in Alain's face.

A. looks at him in disbelief. "You really think you can . . . You must be nuts." He goes for the man's throat.

Apparently he has telegraphed his move, because the man ducks sideways, grabs a shovel and bangs him across the face with it. The creature out cold on the floor now looks like Chet Baker with a bashed-in face.

The area was overgrown with tall weeds. Underneath the Périphérique the ground was studded with turds and strewn with vinyl bags of rank garbage that had been flung from passing cars.

The hot air oscillated between the raw sienna 110 ft. pillars.

There was a campement sauvage nearby. Homeless people and drifters, most of them blacks, had strung tarpaulins between some stunted trees and were cooking sour and unsanitary looking stew over butane flames.

Five of them were sitting around a hookah puffing away. Nobody talked. Nobody played music. There were no children, no birds, no dogs. The only buildings, at some distance, were derelict warehouses and sheds.

When he came to, he didn't feel dejected. Nor was he seething. He found it difficult to think straight when he was seething.

It hurt to move his crushed and swollen lips, but he did, looking into the yellowish bloodshot eyes of his tormentor.

"You want to die? Be my guest."

'What do you call a place like this?" he thought, barely able to suck the stale air into his lungs. It was getting dark. "A null area? No. It's a place just left of center, as you look at the map, in the City of Light. Populated by rejects.'

Before he passed out again he remembered, à propos of nothing, that he had once seen Veronica Lake—his aunt—drinking at the bar of the Morgan after screwing Kate Donovan standing up in the ladies' room. At the Morgan. On Madison Avenue. A century ago.

The three drunk men with Veronica Lake had called her Ronnie.

"It's dealings with women that age people, Jack," she had said to one of them. "That's why priests and queers always look terriffic."

At daybreak the Erinnyas came by, in single file, Ave. C in front, kicking turds this way and that. They didn't look at him.

The turds, both canine and human, glistening with early morning dew like night-blooming flowers. The eastern sky had the unnatural pink hue of denture plates.

The German pope, according to Radio Luxemburg, shot dead in the grotto at Lourdes. No te absolvo, Ratzo. Pendejo.

Any Luck with the Semen in the Girl

There was a stench in the morgue that suggested putrid limbs on a barbecue. Two of the charred bodies were laid out on the slabs.

Heat contraction of the skin of a corpse, according to the pathologist, often produces splits which might be interpreted as tears or cuts inflicted during life.

"So you don't think they were nailed to the wall before the place was set on fire?" The detective didn't want to hear the fine print. To pathologists, cutting to the chase seemed to be an alien concept.

"I didn't say that."

"Good. Any luck with the semen in the girl?"

"No match."

"Pity."

I'll Pull Your Tab, Dybbuk

He didn't remember any of it, but he knew that he had endured worse. He knew it in his bones. It had coded itself into his hippocampus or whatever the thing was called.

So when the hairless ape kicked him in the ribs and indicated that he should mop the floor, he took it in stride.

"I'll just pretend I'm doing it for my Zen master. My wacko roshi with the inoperable brain tumor. Hell, Leonard Cohen did it for eight years . . . " Sure. La vie en rose dans un mauvais quartier. Give it to the singing nun, what's her name.

There was blood—his own—on the floor which had coagulated and begun to smell. He hated the idea of being forced to live by stuff that stank.

"It Appear That the Blood Be Thickenin' . . ." Said Hawk

At first it had seemed that the ape had a way of slapping him around like he was declaring a prurient interest. Imagine having your ass violated by a wheezing deaf-mute with zero body hair. Even the eyebrows are missing.

But no —he had misread the guy, who now seemed to have come around to the view that the role of jailer was a ridiculous burden.

Alain has found a piece of glass behind one of the sacks and has been sharpening it on the cement floor for about an hour, nearly fainting from the exertion. "Say goodbye to your tendons, O Hairless One," he mutters to himself. "I bet you can't wait to see me die of thirst.'

He is sitting just inside the open door of the cubicle, tensing and relaxing the muscles in his arms and legs; he's been doing it for days, but it doesn't seem to help much. Clearly, he is running out of time. And he can't afford to be around when the cops decide to raid the place.

His captor appears satisfied that A. is too weak to crawl away: He no longer locks the door when he goes to sit with the silent drifters and watch their careful spare gestures and confident fatalism.

In the waning light, A. squints across the turded landscape toward the cemetery . . . seems to be a large one . . . would that make it the Cimetière des Batignolles? While the rumble and clash behind him indicates that there must be a railroad yard.

He knows that he is quite dehydrated by now. The skin in the hollow of his knees, he has noticed, is wrinkled and gray.

"Et la nuit se coule dans la vallée comme une longue raie fatiguée." (Sophie Marceau, *Menteuse*)

Licking the half-dried sweat from his upper lip he thinks of the heat smothering Europe in the second summer of the Great Plague. He has already done his Algerian desert mantra. Anything to stay awake. Wait for that ugly Golem to enter his hole in The Concrete to check up on him . . .

He thinks of the heat boiling across the Vieux Port of Marseille, the water black and shiny like an oil spill . . . Oil patches in the streets, and the smell of coalgas. The sky is black and dark green.

He thinks of the killer heat in the Mesopotamian desert. No one goes out except at night when the temperature plummets to 120 degrees. It takes an hour to cross a room.

And he thinks of the attic cells of the prison in Venice from which Casanova managed to escape, across the lead-tiled roofs, having lost thirty pounds to the awful heat in the Fall of 1754.

Yes, and he also remembers, with a certain revulsion, the German actor Gert Froebe in that French made-for-TV movie where G.F., with his wispy red hair and excess weight, has a job scrubbing métro cars at night, and on his way home one morning watches Juliet Berto getting thrown from a speeding car by a pair of hoodlums. She's badly wounded, and he carries her to his place, nurses her back to health, then keeps her prisoner. Must be a French thing.

And Herr F., he remembers it clearly, was wearing an engraved silver ring on the thumb of his right hand, visible as a tracer-like flash every time he hit her in the face.

"From a Distance Even His Shoes Looked Sinister." (Sophie M.)

At 1.30 AM he banged the returning creep unconscious with a shovel. He would have loved to pile cement sacks on him, but he didn't have the strength, so he severed his Achilles tendons. Which was also hard work, with a shard of glass.

At 1.38 he was crawling a slalom through the turds and the garbage bags. ("Traffic-calmed, I see. With huge ugly bollards . . . ")

It took him an hour to get around the cemetery and follow some nighthawks to a Métro station. Which turned out to be closed until 4.30 . . .

They called a cab and offered him a ride to the nearest hospital. He said thanks just the same.

>im in ur base killin ur doodz<

Alain Laurin aka Gerald Lake aka GL23 felt rejected by . . . the planet. Like a plastic net implant supposed to mend a hernia and which the organism has no use for.

He asked Joselito to check him out of the Louisiane. Elvira's concierge, about to go on sick leave, offered to let him stay in her one room plus kitchenette rez-de-chaussée.

"Man, you look awful," she said. "Give it a rest, will you?"

He asked Dr. Denard to make arrangements with one of the A.H. interns to do a quick job on his face, on the cheap.

"I'm out," he added.

"Sorry to hear that."

"I bet you are."

"You do not necessarily have to assume that you went on a

rampage every time you can't remember what you did the other day."

"Well, I do. Just to be on the safe side."

"It could mean that you are getting close. To the origin of your . . . "

"I'm not interested. As in: 'That's close enough, Clem.'"

Vidéo Émotive sur le Suicide

"So you severed his ah Achilles . . . ," says Elvira, back from a stay in a holistic sanatorium in Switzerland.

"It was the part of him closest to the ground. And I was on the ground. À bout de souffle, see."

"Makes sense." She lifts her half-full colostomy bag out of her lap. "Excuse me while I re-arrange my artificial anus . . ." Wearing it openly is her way of making the first move: My shit can be cruel to your shit, so . . . fais gaffe.

"Clearly," she says, "my potential for antagonizing people has increased tenfold."

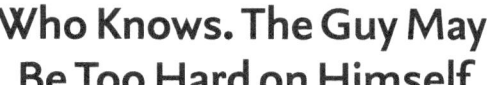

Who Knows. The Guy May Be Too Hard on Himself

How much of a ghoulish character is he compared to the former mercenary who blew up a train station in Angola killing seventy-five people and now seeks consolation in online pornography.

Or the woman of 24 who is tattooed and cut and pierced in every conceivable place and sees pain as part of her "sense of control" of her life. Maleesh.

Or the 60-year-old public accountant in Vermont with a sphincter so loose it made him a viable sex partner for a horse. Which fucked him to death.

Never mind. He needs to be terminated. With extreme prejudice.

"I Say. What's Their Bloody Form?"

"Using the boats left to them by the evacuees of Penang, the Japanese have landed at every port and inlet down the peninsula," he is writing in a dream. He has been waiting for this to re-establish itself in his cerebral cortex. It is the only thing in his life now that feels totally real. He is almost convinced that in a previous existence he's been an Aussie infantryman in Malaya, in 1942.

"We are a hundred miles behind the main Japanese point

of attack on the west coast. It appears that between Parit Sulong, where we are crouching under dense vines and low foliage, and Yong Peng, where we hope to find a British force, lie a fairly high mountain, a large swamp and a great deal of jungle. It is about fifty miles."

A compass, a can of insect repellent, and a deep sense of satisfaction, even gratitude, for having your coordinates straight. For once.

They collected two more sampans and made their way steadily and silently down narrow oily waterways, under leprous mangrove boughs and jungle vines, until eventually they emerged from these slimy tunnels into a broad river. There the Japanese planes searched again . . .

Fresh Out of Virgins, Ahmed

There it is, in the window of La Hune, between the Flore and the Deux Magots. The French edition of his latest effort —*Pas de vierges au Paradis*, by Carol Tanaka. With a red and gold cigar band around it quoting the verdict of The Guardian in orig. English.

"Let's trot out an innocent looking Japanese beauty," says Lansky. "The possibilities are endless."

"Forget it."

"Don't be so stuffy, mate. We've had twenty-thousand

advance orders for christ's sake, let's ride the crest for a change . . . "

Alain waves it away and orders another Mojito.

I wish I could just summon the Sniper, he thinks as he looks at the chatterati planted forever on their rattan chairs around Place St.-Germain-des-Prés.

The ghosts of his victims haven't been around since their defilé under the concrete overpass. It makes no difference. He feels uneasy when they are around and he feels uneasy when they're not.

He knows he probably shouldn't go anywhere by himself now. No telling what he might do, or what others might do to him. What's the choice here —stay indoors or walk around with a bodyguard? Bruno would have to sell motion picture rights before he could afford one. He cares so little it hurts.

He is slow recovering from his latest energy depletion.

He has never drunk so much water in his life.

The critic of Le Figaro, predictably, calls his book the product of a sleazy misanthrope.

Edward Lansky expects to sell in excess of 200,000 copies, Japanese beauty or no.

Duck and Cover Your Entrecôte

Elvira Lansky is in amateur therapist mode. "Have you done irrational things such as snatch a rib steak off someone's plate and sink your teeth in it?"

"Not recently, no."

"It'll come."

"How come everybody knows more about my "condition" than I do?"

"Because you can't know it without acting it out. Compulsively, so to speak."

He has read an entire book about this in the library of the Hôpital Américain. All it tells him is that doing strange and unwelcome things means he's a defective person. Just like the next five or ten people you encounter in the street.

"So? Hide your steak when you see me coming."

"I'll turn over my plate and lean my elbows on it."

La Trahison . . .
Aw Give it to Montesquieu

For cynical relief there was now old man Cordelier, on leave from his news agency job in Washington, D.C. Editions Lansky had, within a month of 9-11, published a book of his predicting a three-pronged attack on the constitution of the United States: By a junta-style gang of civilians in the Pentagon, by manic lawbreakers in the Department of Justice, and by ominous "handlers" of that perceived yoyo in the White House.

The title of the book was *La trahison des jerks.* Sales had been slow but picked up once the Yanks outlawed the term "French fries" and substituted "Freedom fries."

He storms through the offices of Editions L, his hair worse than Don King's, i.e. he's on a roll . . . "And what's the word of caution from dee Press Segatary? 'Always remember —We feed with the pede.' Haven't heard that one, huh? It's what everybody calls the alien in the Oval Office. There are Black Centipede cults springing up in Illinois . . . !"

Head-On Collision of Avatars Fleeing Second Life

Car wrecks are either-or. This one sat dead-center in front of the Alma tunnel entrance. It had crashed down from the road above, but it looked like a metal gob the tunnel had hawked up.

Firefighting foam lingered on the street. The cop cleared his throat. "Medics had to amputate one guy's arm to get him out."

There was litter everywhere —bandages and ripped packaging, caps from disposable syringes, an IV line that had fallen to the ground. Somebody had survived the collision, at least long enough for the paramedics to arrive.

"How many?" The ghost of Detective-Lieutenant Connor, melting through the fog.

"Five dead, four injured," said his Japanese partner.

Crashing down, the Triumph TR4 had sliced through the roof of an airport shuttle minivan. A forensic team was collecting evidence. They were poking at the wreckage as if it was a downed UFO.

The dead woman driver's thigh was shattered so badly that it looked foreshortened. The femur had been driven backward into the pelvis, causing an acetabular fracture typical of car crashes.

And the smell. A mix of gasoline, feces, urine-soaked cloth. Scorched plastic. Exhaust. The metallic tang of blood. The stale tepid scent emitted by mangled flesh.

The police photographer was snapping away. Various angles. The driver's crushed arm nestling in the flaccid airbag. She was forward, twisted around the steering column. Head buried in dash, blond hair fanned out. Passenger equally still, face this way, unseeing eyes half open, pupils blown.

A Blinding Flash of White

He woke at 4 AM, at least he thought he did, and sensed that his remaining will to live was gone. The concierge's place seemed emptied out. Everything was white. He smelled whitewash, glue, hot dust levitating from a radiator. His body felt light as though his bones were filled with air, like those of a bird.

The heat was not the same as outside; it was desert air, dry, with a silicon taste. He walked around, touching the radiators (off), the oven (cold, sort of), the water boiler underneath the sink (off), and he felt strangely confident that he could exist here forever, without food and drink, without a john, without running water, without fuckin' oxygen in fact . . .

And then he remembered with a smile (a smile!) —"In the Land of the Dead, finding a place that serves breakfast is always a problem." (Wm. Burroughs, *Western Lands*)

He is sitting on the black and white tile floor, staring at a stain on the wall. He has been living on tepid tap water for days and can now piss across the floor without creating much of a stink. A purified bladder can be a useful first step.

The stitches in his face are still itching but he has a spray for that.

"You are such a regular Joe" —a remark made by Joselito the other day, half in awe it seemed. Yes, absolutely. He can even feel guilt. He could start cutting himself. He could find him-

self a Hungarian teenager in an internet chatroom —"Let's die together. Jump from a cliff somewhere . . . "

He might get interested in the teachings of Madame Blavatsky. Or Reinhold Niebuhr. Or Russell Braddon of the 18th Australian Infantry.

What's four or five years in a hole in the ground, leading the life of a turnip? It entitles you to nothing. An apprentice Zen hermit on Podunk Mountain will do it on the left cheek of his ass.

Or he can go out and maim the next person that comes his way on Rue de l'Abbaye and get away with it because he has melted through The Membrane and now exists in a parallel universe where true north is thataway.

He has faced the concrete, he has countenanced the torn insides, he has severed and been severed, he's done it all.

"Je vire à gauche, m'éloignant des plantes et des ombres, pour affronter le béton plus cru que le ciel qui l'enserre, massif et dur. Dans la chaleur, les blocs blancs se transforment en vapeur de sable." Sophie Marceau. Make no mistake, she's a better writer than most.

This can be the yield of a brownish grease stain on the kitchen wall of a concierge's place if you stare at it long enough. Then it will be just a matter of acting accordingly.

And old man Cordelier will let an eight-liner from Associated Press spiral down on your casket:

Chino, Calif. (AP) A former slaughterhouse worker has been sentenced to fifteen months in jail and three years of felony probation after being seen sexually abusing sick and injured cattle in a secretly taped video that prompted the largest beef recall in U.S. history in February.

Welcome to the club. "Roulez Francais. Roulez Berliet." A red, white and blue enamel sign on a garage door on the road to Perpignan. Don't park on the lawn. Elle me fout les jetons.

The meaning of life. Must be a French thing. It just came to me. It's you break your ass 24/7 to avoid turning into a full-time cynic.

There it is. We're on to you, Herr Lischka. A/k/a Laurin. La Crim, 38 Quai des Orfèvres. Said to be rather damn good. Fanatics, the lot of them.

Your songlines, eh? The bass solos of Scott LaFaro? You must be nuts. Denied the salt in the air. Un golpe mas y terminamos.

"I was a religious extremist," says the dead woman driver. "It was nun-porn. Bondage, Catholicism, torture. We filmed in an old mansion in the San Fernando Valley."

Joe: I'm driving her back to the hospital. She says don't come to my party. Breaks my fucking heart. Ed's flying in from Copenhagen.

Lost their lives to a coin toss. Roll credits and fade to black. It's been done before.

The room tilted. The pain tearing through him was the worst kind. The last blip on his radar was an image of his face getting grabbed from behind and twisted hard to the side and a knife jammed into the base of his skull, angling up and twisting. There was a sound like empty peanut shells when you step on them at the ball park.

On the receiving end his world exploded white. Death is a ninja. Celluloid scraps on the cutting-room floor swept out by a spectral janitor in the junk-sick morning. A lunger. You've seen him.

In the American Hospital there is a brass plaque on the second floor commemorating the fact that Zelda Fitzgerald had her appendix removed here in June of 1926. "She recovered and returned to the Riviera." They all recovered and returned. It was their specialty. Largest beef recall in U.S. history.

"You never come here anymore, M'sieu Barnes," Madame Lecomte said.

"Too many of us now. Probably loaded with parasites. Cheh!"

> **Les Deux Magots,**
> **Tuesday Sept. 23, 2008. 9 AM.**

*** Coda ***

In the pocket of his 5x8 black Moleskine® notebook, folded several times, yellowed and brittle, there was a half-page from the Los Angeles Times for October 2, 1988 with annotations in Lake's hand in the margins:

The Case: A Special Report
The Killer's Scorecard?

Prosecutors maintain that a paper with 61 entries found in Kraft's car trunk at the time of his arrest is a death list, with entries dating back to late 1971. Killer claims that the list refers to friends of his and to old roommates.

1. STABLE. Wayne Joseph Dukette, 30, of Long Beach, found dead at bottom of a ravine in Orange County, next to the Ortega Highway. Last seen in Stables Bar, Sunset Beach, where he was a bartender.

2. ANGEL. Unsolved.

3. EDM. Edward Daniel Moore, 20, a Marine from Camp Pendleton, found Dec. 26, 1972, at a freeway interchange. Had been strangled three days earlier. Sock stuffed up anus.

4. HARI KARI. Unsolved.

5. AIRPLANE HILL. A "John Doe" found on Airplane Hill in Huntington Beach. Sodomized and emasculated.

6. MARINE DOWN. Unsolved

7. VAN DRIVEWAY. Unsolved.

8. 2 IN 1 MV TO PL. Unsolved.

9. TWIGGY. James Dale Reeves, 19, of Cypress Calif., found near freeway in S. Orange County. Nude except for t-shirt. 4" twig shoved up his anus.

10. VINCE M. Vincent Cruz Mestas, 23, of Long Beach, found at bottom of ravine in San Bernardino mountains. Shoeless. Sock stuffed into anus and genitals mutilated. Hands severed from body. Strangulated.

11. WILMINGTON. Another "John Doe" found Feb. 6, 1973, in Wilmington. Nude with sock up anus.

12. LB MARINA. Unsolved.

13. PIER 2. Thomas Paxton Lee, 25, of Long Beach, found on a pier in Long Beach Harbor, strangled.

14. DIABETIC. Not connected to unsolved murder.

15. SKATES. John William Leras, 17, of Long Beach, found Jan. 4, 1975, floating in surf at Sunset Beach. Wooden surveyor's stake shoved up anus. Was seen the day before boarding a bus en route to a roller skating rink carrying new skates. Suffocated.

16. PORTLAND. Unsolved.

17. NAVY WHITE. Unsolved.

18. USER. Unsolved.

19. PARKING LOT. Keith David Crotwell, 19, of Long Beach. Seen leaving parking lot with Kraft, on March 30, 1975. Severed head found on July 30th near a jetty in Long Beach. Skeletal remains, lacking hands, found that October near the El Toro Marine base in S. Orange County. Forensic specialists matched head to skeleton.

20. DEODORANT. Robert Avila, 16, of Los Angeles, found July 29, 1982, near Hollywood Freeway. Known as heavy deodorant user. Strangled.

21. DOG. Raymond Davis, 13, found July 29, 1982, next to body of Robert Avila, #20. Was visiting relatives in L.A. and had gone to a park to seek his lost dog. Strangled.

22. TEEN TRUCKER. Malcolm Eugene Little, 20, of Selma, Alabama, found June 2, 1974, in remote desert near Salton Sea, California. Emasculated, with branch stuffed up anus. A truck driver had dropped him off in Orange County.

23. IOWA. Unsolved.

24. 7TH STREET. Ronnie Gene Weaver, 20, found July 28, 1973 along 7th Street ramp of San Diego Freeway. Body redressed, except for shoes. Sock up anus. Strangled. Body ejected from moving car.

25. LAKE ANTHONY. (*circled in felt pen*) Not his real name. Approx. 25 years of age; found Sept. 14, 1979 in Big Bear area. Wore military clothing and told people he was a Marine. Body found without head or legs. Emasculated.

26. MC LAGUNA. Roger E. Dickerson, 18, Camp Pendleton

Marine, found June 22, 1974 off a dead-end street in Laguna Beach. Sodomized. Mutilated with bite marks. Strangled.

27. GOLDEN SAILS. Craig Victor Jonaites, 24, found in Long Beach near the Golden Sails Hotel on Pacific Coast Highway. Shoes and socks missing. Strangled with his own shoelaces.

28. EUCLID. Scott Michael Hughes, 18, Pendleton Marine, found April 16, 1978 on Euclid Street freeway on-ramp in Anaheim. Emasculated. Strangled.

29. HAWTH OFF HEAD. "John Doe" found April 22, 1973. Torso on Wilmington. Right leg on Terminal Island Freeway, Long Beach. Head at 7th St. and Redondo in Long Beach. Left leg found behind bar where Kraft worked in Sunset Beach. Strangled. Emasculated.

30. SEVEN SIX. "John Doe" No. 299, found Aug. 29, 1979, in a dumpster behind Union 76 Station in Long Beach. Arms severed at the shoulders, legs at hip joints. Head severed. Only head, left leg and torso recovered. Sock in body cavity.

31. 2 IN 1 HITCH. Unsolved.

32. BIG SUR. Cary Wayne Cordova, 23, of Pasadena, found Aug. 12, 1974, in Laguna Hills. Missing socks and shoes. Cause of death: Acute drug intoxication.

33. MARINE HEAD BP. Mark Alan Marsh, 20, an El Toro Marine, found Feb. 18, 1980, near Castaic, in Los Angeles County, near Interstate 5. Head and hands severed. Large object stuffed up anus.

34. EXPLETIVE DELETED. Paul Joseph Fuchs, 19, of Long

Beach, disappeared Dec. 12, 1976. Last seen at Ripples, a gay bar, in Long Beach.

35. FRONT OF RIPPLES. Unsolved.

36. MARINE CARSON. Richard Allen Keith, 20, a Pendleton Marine, found June 19, 1978, along South Orange County Parkway. Strangled.

37. NEW YEAR'S EVE. Mark Howard Hall, 22, of Santa Ana, Calif., found Jan. 3, 1976, Santiago Canyon. Eyes and genitals mutilated with an automobile cigarette lighter. Emasculated.

38. WESTMINSTER DATE. Jeffrey Bryan Sayre, 15, of Santa Ana, CA. Disappeared Nov. 24, 1979, after dating a girl in Westminster.

39. JAIL OUT. Roland Gerald Young, 23, found near San Diego Freeway, shortly after being released from Orange County Jail for a misdemeanor violation. Emasculated. Cause of death: Stab wound to heart. A jail-release form in his pocket.

40. MARINE DRUNK. Don Harold Crisel, 20, Tustin Marine, found June 19, 1979, on ramp to San Diego Freeway, Orange County. Wearing only shorts. Left nipple burned with auto cigarette lighter. Cause of death: Alcohol and drug poisoning.

41. CARPENTER. Unsolved.

42. TORRANCE. Richard A. Crosby, 20, found Sept. 30, 1978, in San Bernardino County, CA. Route 83. Nipples mutilated with cigarette lighter. Suffocated.

43. MCDUMP HB SHORT. Unsolved.

44. 2 IN 1 BEACH. Geoffrey Allan Nelson, 18, and Rodger James DeVaul, 20, last seen on foot near their homes in Buena Vista Park area, early AM, Feb. 12, 1983. Nelson found that day on Garden Grove Freeway on-ramp. Nude and emasculated. Thrown form moving vehicle. Strangled. DeVaul's body found next day in Angeles National Forest, in a ravine near Claremont where Kraft had gone to college. Sodomized. Suffocated or strangled. Sand on DeVaul linked him to Nelson.

45. HOLLYWOOD BUS. Christopher R. Williams, 17, found Aug. 20, 1981, in the San Bernardino Mountains. Missing socks, shoes, and underwear. Paper stuffed up anus. Known male prostitute who worked from bus stops in Hollywood.

46. MC HB TATTOO. Robert Wyatt Loggins, 19, a Tustin Marine, found Sept. 3, 1980, in a trash bag, nude, on dead-end street in El Toro. Had large tattoo on arm. Death caused by acute intoxication. (*The jury sees a rotting nude youth with hands and feet bound and eyeballs and nipples concentrically scorched with an automobile cigarette lighter.*)

47. OXNARD. Unsolved.

48. PORTLAND ECK. "John Doe," Oregon, found July 18, 1980, near Interstate 5, Woodburn, Oregon. Strangled. Prosecutors cannot connect Kraft's "Eck," but it was listed next to five other Portland entries on his list:

49. PORTLAND DENVER. Michael Shawn O'Fallon, 17, found July 17, 1980 near Interstate 5, Goshen, Oregon. Sodomized. Bludgeoned 31 times on back of head.

50. PORTLAND BLOOD. Michael Duane Clark, 18, found April 10, 1981, near Interstate 5, Salem, OR. Nude. Sodomized. Strangled.

51. PORTLAND HAWAII. Lance Trenton Taggs, 19, found Dec. 9, 1982, near Wilsonville, OR. Redressed. Sock up anus. Taggs' small tote bag marked "Hawaii" found at Kraft's Long Beach home.

52. PORTLAND RESERVE. Anthony José Silveira, 29, found Nov. 28, 1982, on Interstate 5, near Medford, Oregon. Nude. Sodomized. Strangled.

53. PORTLAND HEAD. Brian Harold Witcher, 26, found Nov. 28, 1982, near Wilsonville, Oregon. Thrown from moving vehicle. "Head" on Kraft's list not explained by prosecutors.

54/55. GR TWO. Dennis Patrick Alt and Christopher Alan Schoenborn, two cousins, both found together Dec. 9, 1982, in a field near Grand Rapids, Michigan. Alt missing boots. Genitals exposed. Asphyxiated by choking. Schoenborn found nude, Amway Grand Hotel, pen shoved up anus. Strangled.

56. SD DOPE. Mikeal Lane, 24, of Modesto, CA. found Jan. 19, 1984, nearly a year after Kraft's arrest, in remote mountain area of San Diego County. No clothes with skeletal remains. Drug arrest on his record.

57. HIKE OUT LB BOOTS. Keith Arthur Klingbiel, 23, of Everett, Washington, found July 8, 1978, in traffic lane of Interstate 5, near Mission Viejo. Left nipple burned with auto cigarette lighter. Thrown from a moving vehicle. Death caused by drug poisoning.

58. ENGLAND. Unsolved.

59. OIL. Unsolved.

60. DART 405. Michael Joseph Inderbieten, 20, of Long Beach, found Nov. 18, 1978 at freeway interchange. Nude except for pants pulled down below his waist. Emasculated. Sodomized. Suffocated.

61. WHAT YOU GOT. Unsolved.

May 14, 1983. The night of his arrest. Why was he so dumb. Driving the freeways with a garroted, still warm Marine in the passenger seat. "He was nude and my own pants were down. Still, I insisted that I had found him on the berm and was rushing him to the hospital. I had wiped his genitals as best I could."

They have dubbed him the most notorious killer in U.S. history: Sixty-one men, from ages 13 to 25, killed over a period of ten years. Marines, drifters, dopers, dropouts, stoned along beach and coast thoroughfares.

He has pled innocent, which of course he is. This is Hollywood and he is the King of Siam.

Afterwords

I

At 4:15 PM on the first Sunday in December, 2007, Carl posted a one-paragraph text titled "closeup" to a popular blog service. Subsequently he invited several friends to contribute anonymously to the blog. This must have been surprising. Carl had only begun to use email that year. "Carl blogging?" his friends must have thought. But there was nothing surprising about it at all. Although Carl was a private man who jotted down thoughts and phrases in moleskine notebooks, his entire career as a writer and translator was marked by an uncommon openness to collaboration.

Was the blog a lark? An experiment? A means to learn about the new ways of writing made possible by technology? A way to force himself to move forward with some idea? Likely it was all of these, but it took a while for the project to take shape. That first month, Carl and his collaborators posted a fair amount of text. In January 2008, only Carl posted a handful of paragraphs to the blog. In February, nobody posted. In March, Carl began to catch fire. By the end of the year, Carl had posted—one paragraph at a time—a first draft of the text he would later title *Death in Paris.*

Not that he envisioned it as a book. On November 26, before the text was even finished, he wrote to me in an email, "i will never publish it as a book . . . because of all the stuff in it that is true, but reads like i made it up as i go along . . . " I wasn't the only one excited by the material Carl was generating. Others were urging him to publish it too. As a result, he sometimes wavered about it. We discussed doing a print-on-demand edition to be put out by—he insisted—"Doll No Mori Publishers, Shibuya-ku, Tokyo." The name, which means "Forest of Dolls," was taken from a Japanese manufacturer of sex dolls.

To be honest, I was never entirely clear why Carl was hesitant to publish his text. He himself had posted it on the internet where it was available to one and all. He was concerned about the amount of appropriation in it, yet he acknowledged that his first book, *The Braille Film*, actually contained more: "there is a lot more found material in B Film," he wrote in an email he signed "the cutting edge dim sum eater." To my mind, appropriation was no reason not to publish the text. Carl transcended his sources, turning whatever phrases he lifted into a trenchant new work. But he didn't see it that way. "let's give publishers a wide berth," he wrote me. "if there is to be DiP in book form, i want to do it myself. like, stand next to the printer. and glower. and 'Printed in Japan' is a must."

Carl did agree to let RealityStudio.org publish the text. I pulled together a draft by deleting the other contributors and undoing the reverse order in which the paragraphs had piled up on the blog. Carl took the result, which I had arranged in chronological sequence, and spent the spring of

2009 cleaning it up. For example, he removed that very first paragraph, "closeup," and added the coda. For a few months we had a running dialogue about how the text should look. He couldn't "stand next to the printer" in this case but he was "fastidious" (his word) about every aspect of the editing and design.

It was Carl who found, in an "ancient tourist guide," the picture of the Arc de Triomphe that accompanied the online publication. "The thing is a huge black monster, only seen in outline, there is still the ancient cobblestone street and cars are driving underneath the arc." He and I also had a number of discussions about what to title the text. When he proposed Death in Paris, I objected that there was already a book with that title. For a brief period we settled on We Can Get You Page 776 in the Who's Who of Death. I loved that title but eventually Carl decided to stick with Death in Paris. "Might as well goose Thomas Mann, too, while we're at it."

I was trying desperately to get Death in Paris ready by July 2009, when there was to be a celebration in Paris for the fiftieth anniversary of the publication of Naked Lunch. I thought it would be a terrific moment to launch the text, giving Carl the pleasure of sharing it with so many of the vieux copains who would be there. But unfortunately, because I was planning to post the text at the same time as an archive of materials relating to Carl's career, I couldn't quite get everything ready. In Paris, however, I did spend time with Carl. One night after the cafés closed, I walked him from Île St Louis back to the Louisiane hotel. We were crossing the Place du Parvis Notre-Dame when I thought, "My God, he looks like Rodin's statue of Balzac." Physically Carl did not resemble the statue. But Rodin hadn't been trying to capture Balzac's appearance. He had been trying to capture the writer's vitality, his creative force, and I think that's what I was picking up on. At that moment, wandering toward the quay, Carl seemed larger than life. A writer.

When I returned to New York and Carl to Mannheim, I finished preparing *Death in Paris* and the archive of Weissneriana—scans of books, pamphlets, correspondence, *Klacto*. It went live on RealityStudio on July 24, 2009. Carl seemed pleased, flattered, a little embarrassed. He wrote me that friends thought *Death in Paris* had invented a new genre: "Structuralist Death Metal Pulp." We had another discussion or two about doing a print edition of the text, but Carl continued to reject the idea. Maybe, because he was such a deeply ethical person, he really was bothered by the appropriations. Maybe he didn't want to get bogged down in his own fastidiousness about the details. He had more to write, and it was tremendously inspiring to see how he blazed over the next few years. He published *Manhattan Muffdiver* in 2010, *Die Abenteuer von Trashman* in 2011, and he had other texts in progress when he died in January 2012.

I hate saying "he died" because it sounds like something he did, as though he ate something or he went somewhere. Carl did not die. Death snuck up on him, hit him hard. The unexpectedness of it walloped the rest of us too. In our grief we—Jan Herman and I and a collective mind of other friends—conceived the idea of printing this memorial edition of *Death in Paris*. It seemed like unfinished business. It seemed like a way to help plug the hole in our hearts. If we are giving Carl a bit of the Max Brod treatment, it is because

Death in Paris is a great text and, like Rodin's statue, carries something of the vitality and creative force of its author. To print it is to say that it deserves to endure.

During our discussions about the editing and design of *Death in Paris*, Carl once joked to me about how it had been so long since the appearance of *The Braille Film*. "I see a running text across the bottom (like on Times Sq) . . . 'We are baffled by this guy . . . He writes a book every 40 years . . . Next one in 2049 . . . Assuming the longevity pill —— oh well . . . .'" It is our hope that this memorial edition will serve as a longevity pill of a different sort. Long live *Death in Paris*.

—Keith Seward
March 2012

II

It's no accident that the blog that generated *Death in Paris* was called "The Cutting Floor." Many years ago, when Carl and I exchanged a torrent of letters, he sometimes signed off, "Je coupe tout." It reflected his belief in cut-ups as a method of composition and was characteristic of the texts he was writing at the time. So for his first novel, *The Braille Film*, which I had the privilege of publishing in 1970, the words "Je coupe tout" appear in his handwriting on the author page at the back of the book. They underscored his statement on the copyright page that he had used "variations of the Burroughs/Gysin cutup & fold-in technique" to

write the book. "Consequently," he points out, it is made of "composite texts by many writers living and dead."

Now have a look at the copyright page of this book, where Carl notes, "I am not the author of every line in the book. It is, like *The Braille Film*, a book by several authors, living and dead. One of them myself." But that is where the similarity ends. As consistent as he was in his creative philosophy over nearly half a century, the two books are entirely different in tone, style, and content.

The Braille Film is prescient and panoramic, an extended jazzy riff about a world gone mad. This is the bravura opening: "The passengers of this hopped up mixed media set are on a trip to the end of the nervous system, to the end of the Invisible Environment. There is no guide, no voice, no word." Although German was his native language, Carl had an ear for phrases that made his American English sing. And he seemed to toss it off with the ease and sophistication of a Bill Evans solo.

Death in Paris is more measured. The tone is sardonic and deeply personal, and also very funny, sometimes hilarious. The atmosphere is darker and richer. It is the work of a more mature writer. This time the wordslinging, if you will, is the least part of the story. This time the apocalypse comes wrapped in the jaded formulations of a police procedural, a metafiction that brims with gallows humor.

I first saw "The Cutting Floor" on Dec. 2, 2007, the day it went up. Carl sent me an email inviting me to collaborate on it "directly following its creation this afternoon. It starts somewhere in left field," he noted, "but the ostensible aim is to write a collective militant heathen dissident swansong for the 21st century." I accepted, used the moniker "Cloud9" (his was "Route50"), and posted this item in response:

The agents took the elevator. The doorman keyed them up. Nothing could have prepared them for her apartment. A horn-blowing cherub à la Chagall greeted them from a mural. The living room was supervised by a green-faced Balinese devil with rainbow-colored wings. It sat on a brass sea chest across from a seven-foot giraffe, also brass. Two Chinese Fu dogs perched on the windowsill. "Jiri rented a quarter of my pillow," she said. "It doesn't mean I really knew him." "That's not what the neighbors say," the short one replied. He walked past her toward the windows. Her 12th-floor duplex overlooked Riverside Drive. Rush-hour traffic crawled slowly north. The wind had whipped up white crests on the river.

My blog post ran much longer than that, actually. I wanted to establish my own thread in the story. Carl messaged the next day, "love yr item. peachy. keep it up." I replied, "it will be impossible to keep up w/ your great stuff. ('I SHOULD HAVE KILLED MYSELF WHEN IT STILL MADE SENSE.') Xrist that's good." I posted a handful of other lengthy items, but it was clear to me from the start that the texts Carl was posting—raw, brooding, smartly written, filled with moody details—made "The Cutting Floor" his baby all the way. His posts were so indelible, the storyline and characters so vivid, there was no point in even trying to keep up. Despite his idea for a collective effort, I felt that anything I posted—or, for that matter, anything that anyone else posted—would be interfering. So I dropped out and simply enjoyed the ride.

The ride was all about "your average psychopath who kills women and"—which is not so average—"writes the occasional book." That's worth a heathen guffaw. The fact that this serial killer likes to have sex with a "reusable 'victim'" is worth a double heathen guffaw. That his six-foot inflatable sex doll is custom-made by a Japanese expert to "produce exciting sounds" when being strangled is worth a rictus howl. And how about the "awesome scene in the shy little Wisconsin farmer's home?" That's the way the detective remembers it—"awesome." I can't think of a blackly funnier word with its scent of yuppiedom to describe the "headless corpses hanging upside-down in the kitchen, chairs upholstered with human skin, shoeboxes full of female genitalia." Little wonder that Carl gave the label Doomsday Lit to what he was writing.

In a television interview recorded in Vienna on Jan. 14, 2012, but not broadcast until after his death, Carl spoke about another novel he was working on. He had mentioned it to friends for several years as his Rimbaud-in-Marseille novel, but had put it on hold while finishing *Manhattan Muffdiver* and *Die Abenteuer von Trashman*. When I asked him about it, coincidentally a few days before the TV interview, he replied in an email that he was going to have to go back to Marseille to "earn it," by which he meant he was going to have "to suffer, in situ, endless bad weather bad food bad drinks in crummy waterfront bars first."

Among the books and papers Carl left in neat piles on his kitchen table the night he died—Jan. 24, 2012—there was a 25-page typescript titled "BEBOP IN MARSEILLE," along with several moleskine notebooks that he kept for jotting down ideas, dialogue, scenes, descriptions of places, snatches of overheard conversations, all spurs to his imagi-nation. In one of those notebooks there was this handwrit-ten outline:

The Marseille Stories

On a Monday in June 1961, badly hung over from his birthday party, Karel Schultz, a civilian employee at USA REUR Headquarters (Central Finance & Acctg) in Heidelberg, ~~appeared~~ showed up for an appointment at the university hospital and was told that he had ALS. Amyotropic Lateral Sclerosis. "Unusual for someone your age," they added. "You're what—twenty-five?" "Six. As of today."

The choice was: Absorb a lot of cortisone—a gram a day—and get psychotic and diabetic and wheel around with a puffy mongoloid face; or do a dry run and eventually wither to the shape and brittle-ness of a neglected mummy.

He got his money from the bank, left everything else behind, and took the night train to Marseille.

There, in a cheap hotel by the Vieux Port, he decided to rewrite the rest of his life as it happened, in daily installments, as a novel. One might as well opt for a monstrous task on the way out.

Did Carl have a premonition of his death? I don't know. He was in wonderful humor before he was so rudely inter-rupted. But being "on the way out" couldn't have been far from his mind. On Jan. 7 he had asked in an email, "what do you hear from mustill?" He was referring to the artist Norman O. Mustill, a co-conspirator from the '60s. It was Mustill, in fact, whose motto "Je coupe tout" Carl had ad-opted. "he's got the corragio," I wrote back two days later.

"it's nearly a year since his death sentence. as chipper as he ever was, most of the time. when the pain gets really bad he takes a bigger hit of morphine. says he's turning into a regular junkie." To which Carl replied, "good old norman. i swear i'm going to emulate him when i get hit." Carl had had several operations in recent years, one lasting six hours, which left him feeling as though he'd been "ripped open like a can of sardines." That took an immense toll on his body. He was determined to put it behind him, however, and it appeared that he had. It's heartbreaking to realize now that he hadn't. Although his own monstrous task in Marseille will never be completed, *Death in Paris* was—he earned this one. The "dissident militant swansong" you hold in your hand is the final, graceful proof.

—Jan Herman
March 2012